T0012945

ecstasy

& OTHER STORIES

BIRTH CENTENARY EDITION

ecstasy & OTHER STORIES

THI. JANAKIRAMAN

Translated by David Shulman, S. Ramakrishnan *and* Uma Shankari

PENGUIN BOOKS
An imprint of Penguin Random House

PENGUIN BOOKS

USA | Canada | UK | Ireland | Australia
New Zealand | India | South Africa | China

Penguin Books is part of the Penguin Random House group of companies whose addresses can be found at global.penguinrandomhouse.com

Published by Penguin Random House India Pvt. Ltd
4th Floor, Capital Tower 1, MG Road,
Gurugram 122 002, Haryana, India

All stories first published in Tamil, in different volumes, as detailed on p. 207
First published in English in Penguin Books by Penguin Random House India 2021

Page 207 is an extension of the copyright page

10 9 8 7 6 5 4 3 2 1

ISBN 9780670095964

Typeset in Adobe Caslon Pro by Manipal Technologies Limited, Manipal
Printed at Thomson Press India Ltd, New Delhi

www.penguin.co.in

We dedicate this volume to the memory of S. Ramakrishnan, connoisseur, lexicographer, publisher, and our friend

Contents

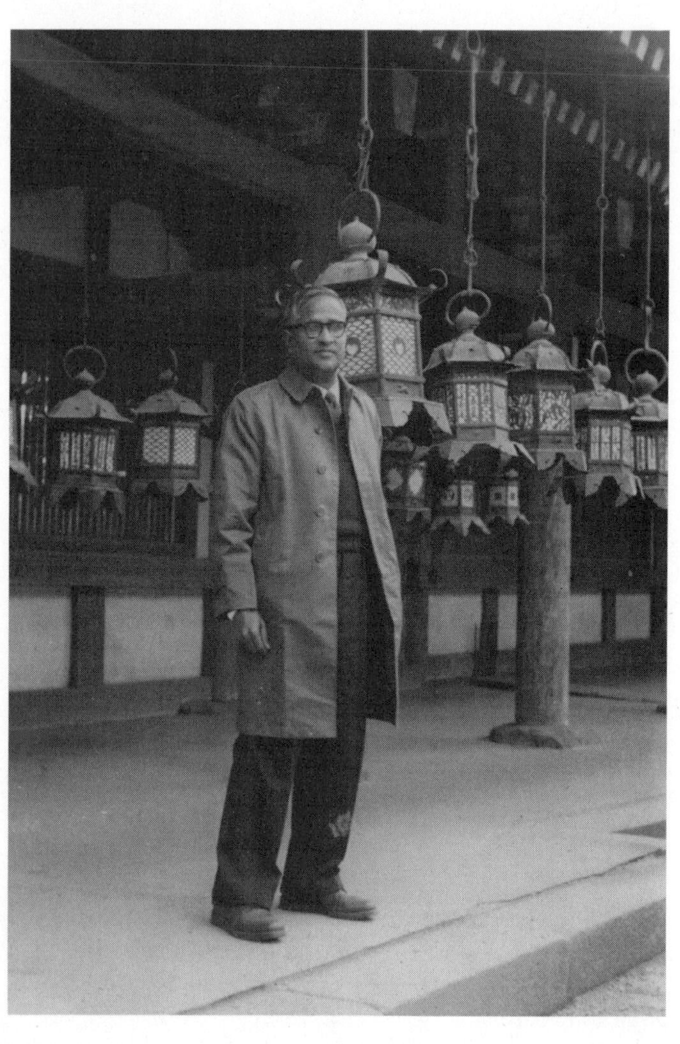

Thi. Janakiraman

Subtleties of the Heart

David Shulman

The author of these stories, known in Tamil as ThiJa or Thi. Janakiraman (1921–1982), was a central figure in the lively Tamil literary scene of the mid-twentieth century. Many would say he was the most gifted of all who were writing at that time. He was born in Tevankudi in the Kaveri Delta and grew up in Tanjavur. Many of his stories are set in the delta; his descriptions of life in rural and small-town Tamil Nadu are almost without parallel. He published over a hundred and fifty exquisite short stories, nine novels, seven novellas, four travelogues, and occasional essays on literary topics. In 1979, he won the Sahitya Akademi award.

ThiJa's father, Tyagaraja Sastri, was a *pravacanam* performer of epic and puranic texts; he was proficient in Sanskrit and in music, a student of the great Mahamahopadhyaya Yajnaswami Sastrigal. The lineage of teaching is important, as it reveals a depth and continuity with the authentic Tanjavur tradition, stretching back for several centuries, of classical music, Tamil and Sanskrit erudition linked to poetic genius, and a particular philosophical orientation. ThiJa, too, was a connoisseur of Carnatic music, and music pervades his writings both as an explicit theme and as the secret of his lucid prose style. He writes a bewitching Tamil, including large segments of reported dialogue (in colloquial Tamil, of course). In one of his essays on music, he writes of the perfect pitch that a true musician demands—and he describes, in an interview, how he has seen his music teacher spend an entire hour, at the start of a concert, tuning the tambura drone to that level of precision.[1] That image would serve well to characterize ThiJa's prose and his uncanny ear for the spoken language. It is far from easy to capture in

English his spare, even laconic style, the insistence on the *mot juste*.

Some Tamil critics have compared ThiJa to de Maupassant, partly because of the way he tells his stories, but also—correctly, to my mind—because of the perfection of his prose. One might also hear a certain Chekhovian resonance, except that in many of Chekhov's stories and plays, very little seems to happen, whereas ThiJa's stories always entail dramatic action. And in terms of the sheer profusion of character, the exuberant social world imagined into being and a constantly evolving richness of observation, ThiJa conjures up Balzac. He read these authors and has written about them; he also translated several works by Western writers into Tamil, among them Pär Lagervist's *The Dwarf* and Grazia Deledda's *The Mother*.[2] Yet, such comparisons, like the always impoverished notion of artistic influence, serve only to veil the singular originality of ThiJa's work and to obscure the nature of his vision. Having mentioned these august names, I can now set them aside for the duration of this essay.

Let me fill in a few more biographical details. ThiJa went to college in Kumbakonam, where he met friends who would accompany him throughout his life. After his BA—around 1939—he looked fruitlessly for a job. He then studied in the Teachers' Training College in Madras and began teaching in schools—in Madras, Ayyampettai, and Kutralam. In 1954, he joined All India Radio (AIR) in Madras, a congenial workplace for him; after fifteen years there, he was transferred to AIR in Delhi as chief producer of Educational Broadcasts for the country. In the course of those three decades, he created countless classic programmes on all topics under the sun. He loved that work, well-suited to his endless curiosity about the world. He retired from AIR in 1982, shortly before he died.[3]

These bare facts cannot in themselves reveal the wholeness and integrity of ThiJa's life or the deeper reaches of his sensibility. Along with Uma Shankari's memoir, we have portraits by his lifelong friends such as M.V. Venkatram and Chitti (P.G. Sundararajan). And if we know how to read him, we can, I think, come to know him, partially yet profoundly, through his own words.

~

ThiJa was a modern writer in all possible senses of that adjective; he would certainly have accepted, or even suggested, this self-definition. The ironies and disjunctions of modernism are evident throughout his work, though always in a personal and distinctive way. He recognized, and went beyond, the feelings of alienation, nameless anxiety, and self-doubt that are the modernist default. No less striking, however, is the palpable sense of his immersion in the specific impulses and ideas of the traditional Tanjavur world mentioned above. That world, like all others, was itself undergoing rapid change during ThiJa's lifetime; inevitably, the awareness of radical change is one of his (often implicit) themes. Yet to my mind, ThiJa was one of the very few modern Tamil prose writers whose minds were not shaped, or perhaps colonized, by the external, sociopolitical forces and ideologies at work in late nineteenth- and early twentieth-century south India. He wrote out of his own direct experience and personal observations, as he himself often said. He was capable of seeing beyond the surface of Tamil life, with its brittle crust of often borrowed contents. I will try to illustrate this.

One easy way to begin is by observing the patterned structure of so many ThiJa narratives. Often, he starts at some point in the middle of his story, with a conversation already laden with bits and pieces from its hidden prologue. Then he swings backward toward that prologue, filling in the missing details the reader needs in order to make sense of the opening paragraphs. At some point, the narrative begins to move forward again, this time in a more or less linear mode, until it reaches a point of crisis, or severe tension, perhaps to be followed by a tentative resolution. Sometimes the story ends without such resolution, leaving the reader struggling to contain the tensile after-effects.

This narration by means of staggered flashbacks is evident in several of the stories in this collection. 'Debt Discharged', for example, that begins with the distress and severe financial setback of a family, proceeds to tell the reader how this situation evolved, then picks up the story from the point where the reader first enters it (in the opening paragraphs) and follows through to a moving and surprising climax. Similarly, 'Alien Note' opens at a point after the story has effectively ended, shifts to a more or less linear narrative beginning far in the past, and reaches a dramatic insight—the real dénouement—before resuming the initial point of departure. Similar patterns—non-linear, zig-zagging narrative segments that nonetheless clearly reveal a causal sequence of events—can be seen in 'The Music Lesson', 'Payasam', 'Message', and other stories. The longer novels are also subject to this style of storytelling, though with much longer digressions and diversions.

ThiJa clearly loved to work like this, but the underlying logic is not a personal idiosyncrasy. Rather, we are seeing a modern variant of a pronounced pre-modern or early modern way of composing a literary (also, at times, a musical or painted) text. There are numerous examples; one telling instance is the sixteenth-century Telugu poet Pingali Suranna's *Kalapurnodayamu* ('The Sound of the Kiss' in the English translation by Velcheru Narayana Rao and myself), in which an obscure, deeply embedded, non-verbal utterance is introduced only towards the middle of the work, though chronologically it precedes and in fact generates everything that has come before. The story as such slowly works its way towards its beginning. In the Kerala classical theatre of Kutiyattam, all plays begin *in medias res* and then move into an extended retrospective segment (sometimes lasting several days or nights) before unfolding in a forward direction towards the end. Artistic masterpieces that fit this temporal mode, or that deliberately shatter the more natural sequence—beginning to middle to end—have good reason to do so. Alternative temporalities and, more to the point, a latent notion of psychic, or intra-psychic, maturation, seek expression along non-linear lines. One might say much the same thing about ThiJa's way of understanding events, usually overdetermined by intersecting causal chains.

It is important to notice that the first passages of the stories tend to be carried along by reported conversation. One enters into the world of the narrative via living speech, which, like all real speech, is pregnant with echoes of the past. ThiJa, in any case, wants his characters to speak to us directly; and, as I have said, he is a great master of what we could call literarized colloquial Tamil. In some sense, these stories are works of oral artistry; it is thus appropriate that many of them are now accessible to us, beautifully read, on YouTube.[4] As a rule, one might say that ThiJa moves his plots forward primarily through reported conversation, with almost no commentary by the narrator.

Then there is the crucial matter of resonant intertexts and quotations. ThiJa cites, or sometimes paraphrases, chunks of text from the Tamil canon, from Vedic or classical Sanskrit, from popular or 'folk' narratives—always to pointed effect. In 'Debt Discharged', when the protagonist's nephew is trying to decode the chain of deceit and theft that has impoverished the family, he says: '*Who is that Kandasamy? Ratna Desigar even doubted that there was such a person. Only God knows who he is. Even He may not know.*' The familiar, everyday setting is graced by the famous verse 10.129.7 of the *Rig Veda*: 'He who created all this—maybe He knows, or maybe He doesn't'. A harsh incongruity in registers generates a savage irony—to be resolved in the shocking end of the story. Both the incongruity and the resolution are hallmarks of ThiJa's visionary mode. Several lines of an ancient Tamil poem from the *Purananuru* anthology (192) are quoted by the policeman hero of 'Offspring': '*We don't wonder at the great or look down at the lowly.*' What are these words doing in this partly comical, partly anguished text? As the story unfolds, they make sense. They have a lot to do with a seemingly lowly cat. Also, the same *Purananuru* poem is famous for its universalist ethic; it begins, '*Every village is my village, every person my kin.*' ThiJa pours an almost unbearable sadness into that thought, which he has brought down to earth and put to work in a Tamil home in some ordinary neighbourhood. This same story, by the way, offers a portrait of the policeman that seems to be drawn directly from the medieval poet Kampan's description of Daśaratha in the *Ramayana* (*Araciyal patalam*) as an upright, tough-minded, and totally effective king.

Here's another, rather unusual example. In 'Payasam', the embittered hero, whose life has been destroyed by envy, goes into the puja room of his house. Once there were pictures of the gods on the wall. Now, however, he sees the paintings of his absent, very modern son:

> He looked around. Madhu's paintings. He studied them closely. He smiled. One painting

> that was only of a leg up to the knee. An eye on top of it. On the eyelashes, a comb. Another painting looks like a young woman, but one leg was a pig's leg. She is tearing her stomach open. Inside there are four knives, a can of powdered milk, and a foetus curled in the womb. Another painting—a lotus flower with a sandal on it. A moustache in the middle of it.
>
> What's all this? His stood there staring, his mind frozen.

I suppose one can take these images as revealing the disarticulated world of the father, no less than that of the painter. Life, especially at moments like the one ThiJa is unveiling for us, can feel surreal and out of joint, even, or especially, in the puja room. But there is an older intertext that turns this passage into a metapoetic comment on the writing of stories or the painting of pictures in general:[5]

> One day, a famous painter came to the court of King Krisnadevaraya and offered to paint a set of murals in one of the royal pavilions. The king agreed and ordered the walls of the pavilion to

> be whitewashed; the painter was set free to paint whatever he wished. When he was finished, the king came, along with the jester Tenali Raman, to see the artist's work—superb paintings of a crowded courtly scene. Krisnadevaraya was pleased. But Tenali Raman objected that one of the painted courtiers was partly hidden by another image. Said the king, 'It's the way we see things. You need an imagination to appreciate great art.' Tenali Raman said, 'I, too, can paint well. Will you let me show you what I can do?'
>
> So the king had the new paintings whitewashed, and Tenali Raman went to work. When the king and his courtiers came to inspect the new murals, what they saw was a strangely conceived and executed set of images—a fingernail floating in empty space; a few specks of dirt here and there; a disembodied eyeball. 'What is this?' asked the bewildered king. Said Tenali Raman: 'Have you forgotten that you need an imagination to appreciate great art?'

I don't know if ThiJa was thinking of Tenali Raman when he wrote 'Payasam'. It makes no difference if he was or wasn't. What matters is that this literally upside-down short story wanted to tell us of its origins, its wider contexts, of what it thinks of its creator (and, I suppose, of what *he* thinks of his creation). The disjointed images of a wayward son reflect back on the author's artistry in a modernist idiom and on his primary poetic means. ThiJa was famously modest about his role as a writer.[6] He seems, for the most part, to have strongly resisted the devilish temptation to tell us about how he worked and what he was trying to say. Not only that, in the long, composite interview published in the Tamil journal *Kanali* in 2020, he was asked about his stories, and he said:

> I'm neither a master of the short story nor a teacher. If somebody asks me to write a short story, my stomach starts churning. Among the hundred-odd short stories that I've written, only one or two come close to what you can call a short story. All the rest of them are almost an insult to that title. If you say to me, OK, then why did you write so much? My answer is: Only the defeated can show you the way.[7]

And yet 'Payasam' is one of his signature stories. It has the psychological acuteness that ThiJa brought to bear in all his oeuvre; also his understated empathy and the sudden revelatory moment of action, as if the agony of the protagonist's mind could no longer be contained inside. In many of the stories, doubt, conflict, pain, and confusion ferment slowly until a point of explosion is reached—and the story can then end, at least in a formal sense. An almost Aristotelian moment of insight and reversal emerges from a chaotic substratum of incommensurable, volatile feelings. Such is the paradox of great art, implicit in the paintings of Madhu and his predecessor, Tenali Raman. Within the space that a writer of genius opens up, there is also room for ethical judgment, or for something we could call conscience, *manasatci* in Tamil. It's one of ThiJa's words (see 'Debt Discharged', 'The Music Lesson', and 'Crown of Thorns'). A humane wisdom nourished by the familiar ambiguity of moral choice permeates his work.

Embedded, expressive reference to prior texts, non-linear sequence, laconic and understated psychograms, the recurrent presence of oral speech—

all these are features of the ThiJa corpus. All of them, including the psychograms, have strong analogues in Carnatic music. Though ThiJa made a decision, early on, not to become a concert musician, and though he chose words as his medium, the musical persona never let him go. We'll see more of it in a moment. But I think we can go deeper, towards the thematic core of his art and the sensibility that informs that core.

~

At subtle turning points, often towards the end of a story, that sensibility speaks to us explicitly. ThiJa knew something about joyfulness; also about sorrow. In that same *Kanali* interview, he says: 'The world around us moves, full of wonders, small and big. To see that is a joy in itself. And that is the root of my writing.' *Viyappukaḷ* are wonders—the raw stuff of reality. Generations of south Asian theorists of aesthetics saw wonder (*adbhuta*, *āścarya*, *camatkāra*) as both trigger and telos of artistic creation. ThiJa connects it (in the plural) to joy, *ānanda*. Actually, we might prefer a stronger translation; we called it 'ecstasy' in the story of that name. Have a look at the final sentence of that text (after reading it through from the beginning).[8]

Few words in the history of south Asia have such a worthy lineage. ThiJa has fully humanized it: it is something that arises in human beings (maybe also in other creatures) in association with a range of emotions, such as the sudden experience of selfless kindness, or compassion, or unexpected friendship, or empathic sadness, as in 'Ecstasy'. It is also, for ThiJa, a concomitant of a wider awareness. Joy emerges from seeing the world under the aspect of wonder. In that respect, in relation to our perceptual faculties, ānanda comes with a sense of wholeness—inside oneself, in the world, and in oneself as a part of or even somehow equivalent to the world. In his daily life, ThiJa cultivated a meditative and spiritual awareness. He was attracted to Jiddu Krishnamurti's teaching. But I think he also knew, from inside, something of the Kaveri Delta version of a personal, individually inflected Advaita, such as we see in the eighteenth-century works of Dharmaraja, among others, and also in the Tantric Srividya, the metaphysical matrix of the composer

Muttusvami Dikshitar's compositions.[9] Dharmaraja (one of several Kaveri Advaitins) offers a theory of perception based on the always singular, individual perceiver (the *jīva-sākṣin* or live witness), who is also partly the creator of whatever object is seen; and in this kind of non-dualism, there is no moment of knowing anything that is not at the same time pregnant with unknowing, with active ignorance. One might think of such a theory of knowledge as belonging to a more general, strongly humanistic, mode of being and feeling.

Note that this highly specific kind of Advaita is not invested in a vision of the empirical world of experience as illusory or, for that matter, even in the assertion of an underlying or overriding unity of being. Nor does joyfulness at this level entail a preternatural tranquillity, *śānti*, as the twentieth-century Neo-Vedantins like to claim. In fact, ānanda in the Tanjavur mode may well be the very opposite of metaphysical tranquillity—a restless disquiet spilling over from the intense thickness and colour and taste of experience, the continuous movement or flow that ThiJa mentions in the sentence quoted above.

Such joyfulness has a rhythm of its own, or maybe many rhythms, mostly slower than our normal pace; it demands patience and a mental space in which to ripen:

> Every experience has to steep in the mind. Something that you have seen or heard has to be turned over again and again. One needs to wait for it. J. Krishnamurthy often calls this 'choice-less awareness'. When you keep circling around a certain event, its truth will blossom inside you. In my experience, this is the only way to bring a story to fruition. If one hurries before it matures and reaches the right moment, it won't be perfect. I know this from practice.[10]

One might characterize ThiJa's stories as always aiming at, preparing us for, and then finding words for the right moment, when wonder happens.

Consider, now, the remarkable story 'Message'. On the surface, judging from the beginning, it looks like a tale of conflict between a classical, conservative, purist musician-father and his son, who is experimenting with film music and other modern inventions. The tension between father and son is certainly important, but that is not what the story is about. It's about music, in a wider sense, and its ability to generate truth—not, however, a single, singular truth. The nagaswaram player Pillai (the father) gives a concert in which an ardent and curious European, Mr Polska, is present. Pillai plays a well-known composition by the eighteenth-century composer, Tyagaraja: *śāntamu leka saukhyamu ledu*, in Sāma raga. Polska, transported, asks the performer to play the composition again and again. Polska then explains, through a translator, what has happened to him:

> The whole world is littered with corpses. There's only noise, shouting, scuffling. A storm fells the trees. Waves rise up and engulf homes. Lightning strikes, and the trees on the road are scorched. Buildings collapse. Wherever you turn, a huge noise. In this battlefield, this tumult, only I see peace. Gradually, the noise abates; the roar of the deluge slowly fades away. A certain peace arises in my heart. The shouting, the clamour,

> the fighting can no longer touch me. I have risen above it all. To a great height, beyond the clouds, beyond the storm, where I don't hear even the slightest sound, where I have discovered peace, an undying peace. That is enough for me. Now I can welcome death. I am ready to dissolve into that peace.

Pillai, astonished, asks the translator:

> 'Peace? That's what he felt?'
>
> 'Yes.'
>
> 'Really? Then isn't that what our Tyagaraja Svami has felt, the peace he sang about in this kirttanam with such yearning?'

We are back in the domain of ecstasy, under a different name—this time, it's called *nāda*, pure sound. As Pillai says, 'Nāda, sound itself, speaks. It crosses all boundaries and delivers the message.' Can we define that message?

Apparently not. The European enthusiast tries and partially succeeds. A gap remains, as we can see from the crucial intertext, the Tyagaraja composition that sparks off this wave of joyful immersion. Here is Tyagaraja's text:

> Without peace, there's no happiness,
> O lotus-eyed Lord—
>
> not even for a person who has overcome passion,
> who knows about God,
>
> not even if you have a wife, children, money, food,
> or if you can chant and fast and so on,
>
> no matter how many texts you have studied,
> not even if you've performed a thousand rituals
> and become famous for your piety,
>
> not even if you know all the subtleties of the heart,
>
> without peace—even a tiny taste of peace,
> Lord of Lords, Tyagaraja's god—
> there's no joy.

That is, of course, only the verbal text. There is something to be said about Sāma raga, too, in particular about the downward cadence with which the phrase *saukhyamu ledu*, 'there's no happiness', is always performed. One should take that melodic segment seriously. There is a difference between peace, or inner quiet—what Pillai calls *amaiti*, a Tamil synonym for *śāntamu* in Tyagaraja's refrain—and the *yearning* for peace (*ekkam*, in Pillai's words). To my ear, the Tyagaraja masterpiece is mainly a vehicle for that restless yearning, a primary theme in the long history of Tamil devotional texts. Singing to the god, Lord Rama, is a way of uttering that very human sense of wanting to be absorbed in Him, of longing for the fullness that mostly eludes us. Or we could say that the song embodies peacefulness in the form of that unquiet yearning. Indeed, this internal tension is the point of the poem. ThiJa used to say that meditation is like short-wave radio music; most of the time you hear noise, now and then you hear beautiful music; but having attained tranquillity even for a moment, the mind yearns for it.[11]

Tyagaraja, at the very end, seems to hint that even God may know such longing. God can offer *upaśāntamu*, 'a tiny taste of peace'. Perhaps that's enough for us, if we get to hear the song.

But what I have just said in no way invalidates Mr Polska's experience. Finally, he finds some quiet in a cacophonous world. (Freedom, said our composer, Tyagaraja, is the ability to hear the seven notes of the scale in the midst of the continuous cacophony of our lives.) I wouldn't want to take away Polska's happiness. Death no longer has any hold on him. But we should notice that the two main parts of this story—the opening disjunction between father and son, and the distinct ways that the European listener and the musician feel the music at the concert—resonate with one another. Polska's epiphany is at once very moving and a little ridiculous, overstated, overdone to the point of irony. Is the nagaswaram player entirely at peace with that revelation? The tone of the narration leaves room for doubt. Not one but two or more messages are being delivered and received.

Radical perspectivism is part of ThiJa's understanding of the world. He loves to show us perceptions of an event, a statement, a thought, a dramatic instant, as refracted through the minds of his various characters. Shifting perspectives are a human truth worthy of meditation and embodiment in art. Sanskrit poetics has a name for the way something or someone is seen differently by various people: *ullekha*, an important ornament or figure, natural to ThiJa's own implied poetics. The Tanjavur Advaita I mentioned earlier—the sense of the put-togetherness of the sensual world—is composed precisely of such interwoven, only partly overlapping perceptions, as we can see in Dharmarāja's uncanny descriptions, mentioned above. ThiJa was skilled in revealing such differences, invariably couched in a loving irony rather than in harsh disjunction, in such a way that a story like 'Message' leaves the reader with an inviting, open space, the opposite of closure.

Still, there is the abiding notion of sound, nāda, at its most delicate, almost inaudible level. Think of nāda as the irreducible reality that enables and expresses joy. There are people who have what is called *nāda pragnai*, the profound awareness of the music that is everywhere around us. ThiJa said that his music teacher, Umayalpuram Swaminatha Aiyar, had it:

> He saw life itself as music. He had a very acute ear. He used to ask us to pay attention to all

> kinds of sounds: a plate falling, noises from the kitchen, a cart rolling in the street. He used to ask us to see how close they came to the basic notes of the scale. This training awakened in me a new awareness of the subtle vibrations of sound, made me sensitive to the hum and buzz that is the universe itself (*nāda pragnai*).[12]

All of this belongs to the informed, attentive, uncluttered mind. One last example: 'The Mendicant' tells of a curse and its fulfilment. The wandering beggar who utters the curse also has something to say about sound and the awareness of sound: 'Sound is everywhere. Are we able to hear it?' The curse follows the flow of sound; a word, even a single syllable, once uttered, cannot be recalled. But there is something more. Apart from his intimate knowledge of the sonar universe, the beggar can see into the human heart, including that of the arrogant and powerful lawyer who mistreats him:

> Your sense of self is so fragile. It doesn't rest on a foundation of love. Cement looks weak. If you mix in water and let it harden, you'll need a

> sledgehammer to break it. Your heart of stone is actually a weak one. If you had mixed even a drop of love into that big ego, it would have stood firm. It would have had the fragrance of jasmine. There's no real strength in your heart.

Many have remarked on ThiJa's gift of insight—another kind of perfect pitch. He has that other kind of knowledge that artists in particular seem to possess, the knowledge of what transpires in another person's mind. That form of knowing, which probably all of us share in some measure (if we don't suppress it), is resistant to our usual, mechanistic, causal explanations. It's a kind of miracle, to be celebrated along with the equally miraculous gift of being able, at times, to see into our own inner selves. In the passage just quoted, ThiJa offers a metapsychology, very Tamil in its formulation. Like the Tamil poets of the Shaiva and Vaishnava scriptures, he thinks the heart is at its best when soft, melted down, fluid, and at its worst when encrusted in solid envelopes.

It wasn't only the human mind that ThiJa could unerringly penetrate. He was also capable of understanding and expressing the mind of other beings such as the Kaveri River, about which (or rather whom) he wrote a ravishing travel book together with his friend Chitti.[13] To read the heart of a river, to perceive her whims and fantasies, is part of that vibrant, personal Tanjavur-based sensibility that colours so much of the ThiJa corpus. He must have refined this gift by his keen listening, by the music that filled him, by his wide reading, by meditation, by his sensitivity to the nuances of everyday Tamil speech. You can also hear it in the surviving recordings of his voice.[14]

This should be enough by way of introduction. You have the stories in your hands or on your screens. I have not touched on several other topics that are conspicuous in ThiJa's writing and that you will see in this volume—for example, his imaginative sensitivity to women, to their suffering as well as to the depth and immediacy of their feelings and their emotional freedom (as many readers have commented). Like other Tamil writers of his time, he was a trenchant social critic. His sense of injustice comes through in his handling of matters of conscience, as hinted above. Many of the stories speak of some tragic set of events, almost always laconically expressed or suggested, as if he wanted, intuitively, to let his readers come to their own conclusions and to feel in their bodies the intensity of his characters' pain—also of the author's pain. But disaster, in a ThiJa tale, is often the trigger for insight that can heal and transform the mind. One is not left with the starkness of tragedy or the unmitigated presence of wickedness. In fact, there seem to be no true, unredeemed villains in the entire ThiJa corpus.

He wrote rapidly, often through the night, and, it seems, rarely corrected what he committed to paper; but he detested superfluous words or syllables: 'Verbosity is heavy baggage. You can't run with it.'[15] He needed to run, and to sing. He filled many pages and left many open spaces. No one should think that the continuities I have pointed to are without their own tensions and complexities, perhaps most evident in those dense silences. As I said at the outset, ThiJa was in all senses a modern writer, a man of his generation and, as such, profoundly rooted in place and time in their continually shifting, often troubling configurations.

As his friend Chitti said, adding to sound and word yet another synaesthesis: 'His writing carries the fragrance of the earth in that place.' In Tamil: *avar ĕḻuttukkaḷil ŏru piratecattiṉ maṇ vācanai vīcukkiṟatu.*[16]

~

This volume has a history. It began when S. Ramakrishnan earnestly requested me to join him in doing a volume of translations from ThiJa's stories, thus continuing our earlier translations from G. Nagarajan (with Abby Ziffren) and Na. Muttuswamy. I happily agreed, and we worked steadily, twice or thrice a week, almost finishing five stories before Ram got sick with corona. His death has left an unbridgeable abyss in my life. We shared many things—friends, stories, words, books from all over the world, music, Chennai. He was forever sending me little bits, or not so little, of Tamil writing and thinking, including the magnificent Cre-A publications and, of course, the evolving masterpiece of the Cre-A dictionary in its several editions. He had a precise ear not only for Tamil but also for English, and we spent many hours searching for the one right word.

His loss cast me into despair. Quite soon after his death, Uma Shankari generously agreed to finish this volume with me. Her direct, deep knowledge of ThiJa, the man and father, helped at every step. She, too, has the gift of hearing the exact nuance. Together, we translated another six stories and went over every word, many times, in the final set of eleven. I hope something of the music of the Tamil comes through. Working with Uma has been a joy.

For me, this volume is a tribute to Thi. Janakiraman; also a memorial offering to my friend Ramakrishnan and thus, so I hope, a debt discharged.

Notes

1. See the memoir by Uma Shankari, 'My Good Father', later in the book.
2. An apparently unfinished Tamil translation of *Moby Dick* has disappeared.
3. It seems that the taped recordings of his broadcasts were erased in order to make room for new recordings on the

same tapes. There was an acute shortage of such tapes at AIR.

4. https://thijastorypark.com/>
5. David Shulman, *The King and the Clown in South Indian Myth and Poetry* (Princeton: Princeton University Press, 1985), p. 189.
6. See Chitti: https://solvanam.com/2011/05/24
   Also Ravi Subramanian in *Kanali*, 13 August 2020: http://kanali.in/anbi-narumanam/
7. Originally published in *Ezhudhuvadhu eppadi?* (Chennai: Pazhaniappaa Brothers, 1969), compiled by Makaram.
8. In 'Ecstasy', the key Tamil word is *cilirppu*, literally 'goosebumps'.
9. See the *Vedānta-paribhāṣā* of Dharmarāja, edited by S.S. Suryanarayana Sastri (Chennai: The Adyar Library and Research Centre, 2003), Chapter 1; also my forthcoming book on *Introspection and Insight*.
10. *Kanali*, loc. cit.
11. Uma Shankari, personal communication.
12. From Uma Shankari, *Mecciyunai (thi.janakiramanaip parri avar makal)* (Hyderabad, 2020), p. 16. See her memoir in this book.
13. *Naṭantāy vā<u>l</u>i kāveri* (Chennai: Bookventure, 1971; reprinted 2017. English translation: *Eternal Kaveri: The Story of a River*. Chennai: Bookventure, 2021). Two other friends, Kalasagaram Rajagopal and C. Srinivasan, joined ThiJa and Chitti for the journey along the whole length of the river.

14. See his final interview on the radio: Bharathi Gnana Thedal - Isai Chithiram by Thi. Janakiraman; date of recording: 26 February1982, https://www.youtube.com/watch?v=fStw3TDq-Wc.
15. *Kanali*, loc. cit.
16. *Colvanam*, no. 248, 13 June 2021.

Temple Bell

The cooking was finished. Margam thickened the sambar with a little flour, stirred it and lifted it from the flame. He put in a touch of coriander, then fried the mustard seeds and added them. The other dishes—a curry of greens and the cooked rice—were also ready.

'Have you cut the banana leaf?' He peeped out into the backyard.

'Yes,' said his wife, handing over the leaves and the knife. She wiped her hands on the edge of her sari and picked up the baby, lying on a piece of cloth on the ground. Holding him in her lap, she began to nurse him.

Margam went to the well and washed off the sweat and grime from cooking. He smeared sacred ash on his forehead, streak by streak, and performed the evening prayer. He returned to the central hall and, sitting near the inner courtyard, began his meditation and chanting. The evening star made a silver dot in the sky. The calf tied in the courtyard stretched its neck and tried to lick him, but the leash was too short. There was a strong smell of calf urine. Margam looked up at the evening star, and the silence of that moment made him feel that he was in the hermitage of some great sage. With one hand covered by his upper cloth while he counted the syllables on the fingers of his other hand, he began to chant the Gayatri mantra. Now and then he closed his eyes. They were closed for a long moment when he heard someone slipping off his sandals. Margam opened the door and said, 'Come in.'

'Dinner . . .' asked the guest, drawing out the word.

'It's ready, come,' Margam said, and hurriedly finished his prayer, placed the wooden plank for him to sit on, and put down the banana leaf.

The guest was very hungry. It showed in the way he ate. He was not a regular customer. He would come once or twice a month. Margam knew only that he lived on Temple Street and worked as an assistant to the science teacher in the local high school. When you looked at him, you felt sorry. His very appearance aroused pity. He was short and a little chubby. On his round, bald head, you could count five or six grey hairs like the whiskers of a cat. Silver-framed glasses on his nose. His right eye looked big through the glasses. He wore a rough, khaki-coloured shirt with short sleeves. Even his walk was like that of a child—step after step while trying to look straight ahead. The science room in the school faced the street. He would sit near the window and stare at the street like a sage. Whenever Margam looked at him, for no particular reason, pity would well up inside him.

That's why even though he came only once or twice in a month or two, Margam would feel as if the silent sage Jadabharata or an ascetic had arrived, and he would joyfully and respectfully serve him. Usually, if passersby happened to hear the sounds coming from inside, they would think Margam was pouring serving after serving of rice; unless they went inside, they wouldn't understand. He would bring the rice in a brass plate with a dent in the middle. It was there for a reason—it stopped the rice from slipping onto the leaf. He'd rush into the hall and serve the rice while making a big show, tapping on the brass plate. But the rice knew who was the boss. It would fall on to the leaf bit by bit. Not only the rice—the curry, dal, ghee, even the dishes knew who was in charge. The plate and the ladle would rattle as if to say, 'I'm making so much noise, why don't you pay attention?! Are you so deaf that you ignore the racket in order to get your fill?' Margam, taking advantage of the customers' reticence, would serve the ghee with tweezers and the dishes with a tablespoon instead of a large ladle; also the pickle with the handle of the teaspoon. Why go on about it? You can't go to this 'hotel' expecting a lavish dinner. You have to realize that you'll be getting 'homely' and dietetic food.

Only for this man did Margam make an exception. The plate and the ladle knew it, too. You should have heard how they became silent and humble.

He ate well. He praised the sambar and asked for more to go with the curd rice. After serving him, Margam, by chance, stirred the sambar and lifted up the ladle. Something had fallen into the sambar. He stirred it again and looked closely at the ladle in the light. What was it? Something long and smooth, its shiny skin dulled by the heat. Was it a baby snake? A lizard? Lizards have feet; this didn't. It looked like a baby snake. As a moving cloud casts a shadow on the ground, a shadow passed through Margam from head to toe. Just a shadow. What else can we say? Was it fear, or terror, or worry? Who can say? A shadow. He signalled to his wife. He showed her the creature in the ladle. Her eyes widened. Her mouth dropped open. She covered it with her hand. Margam also covered her mouth with his left hand. Her breathing came fast. A tremor went up to her head. She steadied herself, taking hold of a pillar. Yes, it was a baby snake.

The old man finished eating, washed his hand, belched, put on his sandals, and groped his way out. She watched him go. The next moment, with the ladle in her hand, ignoring the darkness, she walked to the far corner of the backyard and threw the snake on to the pile of rubbish. Then, still terrified, she threw fifty or sixty fistfuls of mud and rubbish over it. She came back inside, took the sambar and poured it into the gutter.

'Will something happen?' she asked. Her voice got stuck in her throat.

'God knows,' said Margam, on the verge of tears.

Shackles, prison, curses—she saw them all. Her hands trembled.

'We'd better pray.'

~

The two of them stood in their puja room before the pictures of the gods.

'We have lived with dignity for so long. Why are you putting us to this test?' She wept, looking at the gods.

'I promise to donate a big bell made of the best alloys of five metals, as big as my arm. Keep the news from spreading, Yugesvara,' Margam prayed.

His wife heard him. 'God,' she said, 'no other ear should hear of this. We'll have a big five-metal bell made for the temple. Oh Lord, Yugesvara, Lord of all, Friend of the Weak, Margabandhu, Friend for the Road.' Even in the midst of her rush of feeling, she felt a little shy at having uttered her husband's name, the same as the Lord's.

They made a new kettle of sambar from kummatti fruits. The regulars—all twenty-four of them—came and had their dinner.

However much one prays, do doubt and fear go away? Margam couldn't sleep well at night. Only his wife, handing over the burden to the god, slept peacefully.

Margam tossed and turned. He felt like going to Temple Street to have a look. What sin had he committed that brought about this negligence? Was it the hot sigh of those who ate without filling their bellies? Nattani, the motherless son of Vempu Aiyar, of the yarn shop, said with a boldness that no one else had, 'Why are you serving me like throwing grains at little chicks? You have to give value for the money you take. It's just greasing the lining of my stomach.' Sitting in front of the banana leaf, he was burning with anger.

The next morning, news reached Margam that the science teacher's assistant had died. He had gone to the backyard twice during the night, drunk some water, lay down again, slept, and didn't get up. The doctor declared it was a heart attack. The whole town said so. If it were possible to find reasons for all the crimes in the world, and all the criminals, every house would be a prison.

Yugesvara had saved him.

~

Within a month, the temple bell was ready. Made of five metals. A weighty bell. More than half an arm's length. You needed two men to lift it, straining hard. It was magnificent to the eye, and the sound even more magnificent. The coppersmith who cast it was no ordinary craftsman. His name was Vaittilinga Acari. How did he produce such beauty? His workmen brought it and left it in the courtyard. Margam couldn't take his eyes off it. The bell sat there, proud, very dignified. It looked a bit like Shiva's bull. Or like a handsome Andhra princess. Sometimes, it even looked like the entrance tower to a temple. The coppersmith had applied some white lime on it; and along the rim were inscribed the words, 'Offered by Margabandhu'. It was as if the voice of Lord Yugesvara himself, who protected him from shame and trouble, had taken on form. The force of the Lord's compassion resounded in silence.

It cost just six hundred rupees. Margam saluted Engineer Appasamy. For twenty-five years, Margam had cooked for Appasamy's family. In the end, Appasamy gave him a grant of three thousand rupees and blessed him, telling him he should start his own business. It wasn't in vain. Margam had married off his daughter well. He got his son educated; he was now working in a bank in Madurai. Afterwards, there were four or five miscarriages, and, now, one child was left, weak and ugly as a monkey. It was OK that some great good fortune didn't shine on him; the Lord of All had saved him from shame and embarrassment. What is six hundred rupees? He would have given six thousand.

Among the regulars, not one failed to marvel at the bell. Who would think of having a bell made for the temple? People make all kinds of offerings—metal eyes for the god's image, a garland of vadai doughnuts, a pilgrims' guesthouse, sandalwood paste to be applied to the stone icon. But who would offer a temple bell?

Margam would modestly reply to those who asked: 'Just like that. The thought came to me that I should make something for the god.'

Those who came to eat would caress the bell; tap it with their fingers. Some tried to see if they could move it a little.

'It's beautiful to look at,' they said, staring at it.

'Such a pious act. How did you think of it?' some asked eagerly.

'Since God takes care of us all the time, how could I not think of it? People drop dead just like that. God holds us in the palm of his hand at every step we take. Somebody asks for water, and before the water comes, he's dead. Who keeps us alive? I'll give you an example. You know Airavatam, the assistant at the school? He came here and had his dinner the night before he died. The next morning, he was gone. The doctor said it was a heart attack. If he hadn't said that what would people say? That fellow who had dinner at Margam's, the next thing you know he has kicked the bucket.' Margam spoke, his nostrils flaring, his mouth filled with tobacco. Worried.

'Oh no, who would be crazy enough to say that?'

'Not like that, sir. Even then, what do we know? I was just saying.'

He went on. 'Everybody knows Margam. But who knows what people will say? Who can say what will happen when? The times are like that! Airavatam used to come to eat from time to time. I used to be worried when I saw him walking. Whenever he came to eat, I'd feel it in the pit of my stomach. I used to pray to God that he should reach home safely. I saw how weak he was, and it scared me.'

His wife spoke up from inside. 'Are you going to be talking forever? The rice is getting mushy. You'd better take it from the stove.'

Margam stood up and went in. 'I'm coming.'

The customers left.

'Look. Go take the bell to the temple. When I listen to you, my stomach starts churning with worry.'

'What is it that I said?'

'Whatever you said so far is enough. First take the bell to the temple. People are asking about it just because it's sitting here. And you can't help talking about it.'

'Do you think I'm such a fool?'

'You're a smart man, but just take it there.'

'They have set an auspicious time.'

'Yes, for installing it, not for bringing it.'

~

That evening, the bell reached the temple. Two days later, on a Friday, it was put in place on a raised platform. They tied a rope to it and told Margam to ring the bell. He did.

Ding dong . . .

It took a whole minute for the sound to fade away. He sat on the platform as his mind disappeared into the emptiness along with that resonance. He had closed his eyes. Startled, he opened them when someone pulled the rope again and produced that sound. The rope was in the hand of the temple trustee.

The bell rang four times every day—in the morning when the god's full form was revealed, at noon, in the evening, and at night.

At home in the morning, just like when he was in the temple, Margam closed his eyes and melted into the sound, absorbed in space. It was the same at noon. At sunset, as usual, he sat in prayer in his courtyard. He could see the sky. The evening star had not yet come out. The sound of the temple bell floated toward him like golden smoke.

'Is the food ready?' He heard the voice and the shuffling off of sandals. Airavatam peeked in, wearing his khaki shirt, one big eye behind his spectacles, with his cat's whiskers and his bald head.

Margam was shocked. There was no one in the passageway. Airavatam had died a month and half ago. Margam shut his eyes tightly. How could one keep Airavatam from coming back on the waves of the temple bell? Airavatam is not asking for his dinner now. He is lying on the waves, bobbing up and down like a log in the sea. Not him, but that thing. It isn't Airavatam, it isn't his body, and it isn't the sea. It's just a wave of that kummatti sambar. Margam felt an icy chill, a crackle in his spine. He opened his eyes and stood up. He went into the kitchen and stared at the wood stove, his hand on his waist.

He heard his wife's voice. 'Why are you standing there staring?'

'Mm.'

'I've been watching you. You're staring at the stove. What's there?'

'Nothing.'

She came close to him, looked at his face.

'What are you seeing?'

'Nothing . . .'

'Then why? . . .' She went to the puja room, took a pinch of sacred ash, and smeared it on his forehead.

'I believe you donated the temple bell?' asked the bookkeeper from the grocery store.

'Yes.'

'Hm. What a sound! I've heard the bells at Tiruvarur and Malaikkottai. They don't have that same resonance, wave after wave.'

'Like the coils of a python, isn't it?'

'Yes, yes. Like a really big python. The sound is like that. Thick and heavy.'

'Like Takshaka, like Vasuki, the famous snakes.'

'Who are they?' asked the bookkeeper.

'Takshaka bit King Parikshit and killed him. Vasuki wound himself around the Mandara

Mountain as the churning rope when the gods and demons churned poison and nectar from the ocean of milk.'

'Right, I forgot. That Vasuki!'

'So you're saying that other temple bells are like baby snakes, and ours is a python,' said Margam.

Margam's wife interrupted. 'Shall I serve the food?'

'Why not?'

'I'm a little busy. Come here.'

Margam went inside.

'Why are you two talking about Takshaka and Vasuki? At night it sounds scary.'

'He didn't say it, I said it.'

'Okay, okay.'

The bookkeeper finished his meal and left.

At ten o'clock in the night—again, that mighty sound. The midnight service in the temple.

Margam was lying down. Every now and then, he would lift up the old mattress on his nuptial bed and peek under it. Then he'd lie down again.

'What's there?'

'Where?'

'In the courtyard.'

'Nothing.'

'No. Look, it's moving. Bring the lamp.'

As soon as he held up the lamp, the thing disappeared. When he put the lamp back in its place on the wall, it appeared again.

'Look at it!'

His wife looked, like following a bird in flight. She cut away a piece of string hanging from a pillar.

'It was just the shadow of this string.'

'My God, I got scared.'

After that, too, he couldn't sleep. He turned up the wick of the lamp.

Lay down again.

His wife and the child were sleeping soundly.

A cow mooed. Is it already milking time? He hadn't slept a wink.

Again, the bell for the morning service.

Margam got up, brushed his teeth. His mouth full of betel and tobacco, he went to see the temple trustee.

He was sitting on the pyol, chatting with one of the workers. His wife was sprinkling cow-dung wash at the entrance to the house. 'Come,' he said. 'Everyone who sees the bell has something to say.

This man spent the night in Ammapettai village. How many miles away is that? Nine stones . . .'

'Yes, sir. What a sound! Booming like mad. I even told my nephew. You know what, you lowly Dalit.[1] We've become Christians. But when I heard that bell, I wondered why we did that.'

'Wow. Well said. Did you understand what he said, sir? He has been a Christian since his father's days. Now, after hearing your bell, he feels like changing back. Isn't that so?'

'Yes, indeed.'

'I came to talk about that,' said Margam. 'Whenever I hear the bell, I begin to feel conceited . . . that I'm the one who brought it. That's wrong, a big problem, isn't it?'

'What are you talking about, sir? People who donate even a garbage bin brag about it with drums in the streets. They produce a long inscription about it.'

The trustee's wife had begun drawing the threshold design with rice flour—all dots and zigzag lines.

'Somehow I don't feel at ease with what I did. There are so many big people. I feel it's an impertinence on my part. Every time I hear that bell ringing, that feeling comes to me. That's why I had another idea. I came to tell you.'

'What's that?'

'I thought I'd have four small silver bells made for the same price. One for Pillaiyar. One for the Lord. One for the goddess. And one for Subrahmanya. I'll take back the big one.'

'What are you saying?'

'Yes, sir. Who am I anyway? I'm just a small fellow tucked away in a corner.'

'By all means, make those silver bells. I wouldn't say no. But how can you take this one back? My Lord himself entered your heart and moved you to make this bell. . . . This is too much. Anyone who hears your new plan will laugh his head off. People will wonder if you've lost your mind. For *this* you rushed over here at the crack of dawn? Didn't you hear this guy say that he wants to reconvert?'

Margam went white.

The more he talked with the trustee, the more stubborn he became.

Margam went home, sad and weary.

While he was taking his bath at the well, the bell rang again in the morning puja. It hit him hard. He tried to imagine what it must feel like to be totally deaf.

Note

1. Literally, someone (from a low caste) who has to drink from a separate glass or cup.

Alien Note

Dear Sir,

The letter of condolence you sent to my mother arrived.

> Your husband Sri Balaraman was famous for his profound knowledge of music. He was a connoisseur of the first rank. His music criticism, without fear or favour, was proof that he lived and breathed for music. The world of music is steeped in grief at his departure. Our Bhringi Music Club sends you and your children deepest condolences in this dark hour of loss.

So you have said in your letter.

Mother read your letter and sat, staring, for some time. I asked her if I should send off a thank-you note. She said, 'This letter is all wrong. Why don't you write a detailed reply?' She stood at the door and asked, 'Do you think that letter is okay?'

I read it again, weighing every word. I felt that almost nothing was right. That's what I said to Mother. 'In that case, better demolish those lies,' she said as she went out.

I read your letter once more. I smiled at Father's cunning. He managed to throw dust in the eyes of even the harsh critics of the Bhringi Music Club. Father was no connoisseur and no scholar of music. In fact, he passed the time in constant fear. His passion was not music but food. Father could distinguish twelve subtle varieties in every flavour, just like all the technical terms that the musicologists use—the seven notes of the scale, their sharps and flats, the microtones, the pitches. For him, the ultimate goal of life was to eat. I don't know if there was any love between Mother and Father. If there was any, it was nipped in the bud. Neither Mother nor we children are groping in the dark. I'm studying an honours course with home science and music as my special subjects. My brother has a job as a chemist in a company. He and I are living in Vile Parle in Bombay. Mother is living happily in Goregaon with her loving husband—the present one. She's not Father's wife. Only when they came and took Father away to the mental hospital did Mother find relief. Three years later, she got legally divorced.

They say that the sins of the father and mother fall upon the children. My father bore that sin on his head. In the end, it seeped inside his head. The mistake his father, my grandfather, made was to try to teach his son music. His mother's, my grandmother's, mistake was to not stop my grandfather. That's why sometimes when I think about Father, I feel sad.

Grandfather had three sons. The first two sons sang beautifully. Grandfather was the principal of a school; he was also proficient in music. Not only did he know music; he was constantly swimming in it. When he heard his sons sing, he was ecstatic. He had vowed to himself that as soon as his sons were old enough, he would introduce them to the grammar and aesthetics of music. But something happened that broke his heart. The first two boys had gone swimming in some ordinary river, and the river took their lives. Their bodies were found far away. Grandfather couldn't bear his grief. To whom could he bequeath all his wealth of musical knowledge? Only to the third boy. There was no other heir. So when Father turned seven, Grandfather started teaching him music. Life is short, so there was great urgency in teaching him all the textbooks and history of music. Although Father couldn't sing, he could memorize well—even the very big books. If anyone asked him, he could reproduce anything verbatim. The only thing he couldn't do was sing. Grandfather used to beat him with anything at hand—his palm, his fist, a nutcracker, a book, a glass. He would shut his eyes and pound Father with any weapon. In this way, his training went on for a long time. In the meantime, Father got married. But his training continued along with the inevitable torrents of abuse. To no effect. How can anything sprout in a desert? All the music texts that he had memorized were like manure on a stony patch of earth. Music didn't take root. Grandfather would sigh in weariness. 'You're like an alien planet,' he would say in exasperation, coining a new term. 'Where did you come from?'

Mother used to hear this. She was a young girl. The marriage had not yet been consummated. In those days, it was the custom that a young bride would shuttle between her parents' home and her husband's. She had no idea what 'alien'—*bhasanga*—meant. She thought maybe it was from *pashanam*, 'poison'. One day Grandfather called him 'You devil of an alien note, go hang yourself.' With this blessing, he put an end to Father's music lessons.

Grandfather didn't live long after that. One day he left this world. By that time, he could no longer sing. On his deathbed, looking at his son, he wept.

Father cried like a little boy when Grandfather died. He kept trying to understand why Grandfather shed tears towards the end when he couldn't speak. Then he understood. He must have been grieving for his shattered dreams. From that moment on, Father didn't go to work. He took a decision. He would work only for the sake of music.

Father started talking music. He would speak at home. He would speak about it outside. In the restaurant. At the railway station. With friends.

If someone insisted that he come to a concert, he would sit outside and talk about the music. Now people began to be afraid of him. The musicians would run away and hide from him. 'Let him go where he wants, so long as he doesn't pounce on us.' But that didn't mean he had no friends. Four or five people like him always hung around him. Who would desert someone who has money? He would also bring them home for meals. Two fried vegetables, two curries, sambar, pitlai, fritters, and payasam—Mother would lay out all of this. She didn't mind the cooking, but what drove her mad were Father's grinding voice and the voices of his friends. Occasionally, Father couldn't resist singing himself. When that happened, Mother would pale as if she'd seen a ghost. Whether his friends came or not, Father had to have at least four dishes at every meal. And the appalam had to be fried, not roasted. Every day: at dawn, a plate of idli or pongal with coffee. At 8:00, another coffee. At 10:00, another coffee with two biscuits. Lunch at 12:00. At 2:00, more coffee. At 4:00, tiffin and coffee. At 6:00, another coffee. Dinner at 8:00. At 10:00, a cup of tea. At midnight, ginger and coriander coffee with snacks. In between, he'd get snacks from a restaurant. Mother was terrified that a person could eat so much. Little by little, that fear turned into panic: how could she go on producing so much food? After all, Father's money didn't grow on trees. All his assets—his provident fund, the house in the village, and the agricultural lands—were eaten up.

Father started writing to musicians. He sent letters to a hundred-odd persons saying, 'I can count on my fingers the number of musicians who can sing like you.' Some of them came to thank him in person. To some he went himself. What for? To borrow money. That worked with about twenty of them. But, meanwhile, when musicians would get together, the impression each of them had—that Father had written only to him—was exposed for what it was. Once they had been afraid of him—now they began to laugh at him.

The elaborate lunches and dinners were reduced to one curry and a soup.

Father started teasing Mother: 'What's going on? We're eating like in your father's home.'

In fact, Mother was indeed bringing supplies from her father's house. How long could that go on? Were her parents going to live forever? They also passed away. Even if her brothers were willing, would their wives put up with it?

'Do you think I'm like your father?' he would go on nagging her.

One day he said to her, 'Your father used to complain that I had no real interest in making money the way he did. Even if I didn't make money, there was no dearth of people coming and going. I was as important as ten rich men. So your father was jealous and frustrated. Up to the time he died, he would make these snide remarks. Now his soul must have attained peace, as I'm truly having a hard time.' When Mother heard this, she started sobbing uncontrollably. She'd put up with it for a long time. Then one day, as if she was possessed, she let out a huge scream. 'That's enough! Don't ever talk about my father again!' You could hear the cry from across the street. Father was shaken. He stood in silence for a while. Then he went out.

From that moment on, Mother became an ordinary woman. Until then, she had been like the model wife that the books describe, with all the duties of a housewife. Suddenly, she stopped and turned into a woman like other women.

That's when Vijayaraghavan became Father's friend. He was never sloppy like Father. He didn't wear unwashed clothes. He didn't tease. He didn't eat all the time. But still he was Father's friend. One day, he was chatting with Father in the hall.

'Sir, how long can you go on like this? Why not find some way of earning something?'

'What am I lacking? I'm happy.'

'What about an income?'

'What about it? I'm fighting for the truth. People like me die in poverty. You'll know if you study the history of the arts.'

'You got married, produced a family . . .'

'What can I do about that? If they don't have the strength to bear it, what can I do?'

Amma was making coffee inside. 'Damn you,' she said. Just that morning, Vijayaraghavan had brought a big packet of coffee powder.

'But you have received a lawyer's notice from four different creditors.'

'Let them be. If I have money, I'll pay them back.'

'Shouldn't you be making some effort to return the loans?'

'Vijayaraghavan, I never borrowed the money with the thought of returning it. That kind of bloody honesty applies only to ordinary people.'

Mother felt like puking.

'But this is true only for great artists and geniuses.'

'So, you're implying that I'm not an artist. What difference does it make what you think?' Father said.

'Give this coffee to Uncle,' Mother said to me. I took it to him.

Father yelled, 'Rati, there's no sugar in it.'

I picked up the tin of sugar, but Mother said, 'Put it down!' She took up her position at the door. She laughed. 'Does a great artist need sugar?' I was perplexed. Why did she laugh? It sounded more like thunder in the silence of the night. Mother went back into the kitchen.

One day, I was sitting in the veranda near the kitchen, reading. Mother was talking to Vijayaraghavan Uncle. After half an hour, I heard Father's voice. Mother went inside.

The voice said, 'It seems you've got wind of a good deal here.'

I heard Vijayaraghavan Uncle say, 'What?'

'It seems you come here when I'm not around.'

'What if I do?'

'What did you say? Get out!'

Amma came to the door. So did I. Vijayaraghavan Uncle didn't get up from his chair. He was staring at Father, like studying a millipede or a spider. Father looked at Mother. He rushed out without even putting on his sandals. Vijayaraghavan Uncle was sitting there like a wave in a painting of the ocean. After five minutes, the wave moved. He got up and left.

Father came back at 6:00. He went into the kitchen.

Staring at the walls, he said, 'So you knew I'd be back.'

Mother said, 'No need for this crazy talk. Today we have to decide one way or another.'

'Is that so? . . . Why does Vijayaraghavan come here so often when I'm not around?'

'Why? Shall I tell you?' She smiled out of one corner of her mouth.

'You're threatening me.'

'That's *your* job. I'm not a musician. You can't scare me. Now it's your turn to be scared.'

'Don't keep threatening me. Tell me why he comes.'

'Why does an alien note come into a raga?'

'. . .'

'Tell me why it comes.'

Father drew himself up. He kept staring.

'Go ahead, tell me,' said Mother.

Quietly, he said, 'For the sake of beauty.'

'Do you understand now? Why the alien note? It's there to bring beauty to the raga. It nurtures the raga. For the last four months, Vijayaraghavan has been caring for this family. For these four months, the food you ate and the coffee you drank all came from him. Though you've studied all those books, you haven't understood that there is an alien note in this house.' Amma shrugged her shoulders, mocking him.

Father hit himself hard on his head and face. I tried to stop him. Mother said, 'Don't.' Father kept on pounding himself. 'You and your daughter are both alien notes, you heartless woman!' he said, grinding his teeth. He went out again.

Madness seized him. He would come and shout from outside the house. 'Don't sing those alien notes. It ruins the family.' He would rip his soiled veshti. By chance, Father's cousin came down from the north and saw the situation at home. He took him back with him to the north, where he had a job. First, he called in the local exorcists, but it was no use. Then, he had him admitted to a mental hospital. Father could not be cured. He was in the hospital for five years and died there. His cousin was very fond of him, as cousins are. He must have placed the obituary in the newspaper. That's how we, too, got to know. Your condolence letter bears post office stamps from all over. It finally arrived the day before yesterday. One month after his cousin took him with him, we shifted to Bombay.

Please forgive me for writing such a long letter. People say there is a thin line between genius and madness. But since you seem to be confused, as if there *were* no line, I had to write this letter, with Mother's permission. One should not write such things about one's father. What to do? It's very sad. But the suffering my brother and I went through because of him . . .'

Yours,
Ratipatipriya

P.S. Mother came today from Goregaon. I showed her my reply. She wants to add a few words.

Namaskaram . . . Everything my daughter said is true. But before Balaraman went mad, something happened. The doubt he had about me and the rage and confusion did not stop him from coming on time for every meal. It was only afterwards that I wrote to his cousin and asked him to come. . . . What my daughter has said is very true. He bore his father's burden on his head. What fault was it of ours?

Yours,
Vijaya Vijayaraghavan

Offspring

The conch was blowing. Mudaliyar stood up quickly and went to look out the window. At the house opposite, thirty to forty people were ready to set out. Just outside the gate, the conch player, a short fellow with a turban on his head, was puffing up his cheeks and blowing the conch. In the midst of the crowd in the compound, Muttaiya's eldest son, dressed in a white silk veshti and with a white turban on his head, was holding in both hands a big plate covered with a white cloth. A spathe of coconut flowers was peeking out from below the white cloth. The younger son, Ellappan, was standing beside him, dressed like him. Ten or twelve days had passed since Muttaiya had passed on. The crowd was setting out to perform the final funeral rites.

The conch player moved ahead. The eldest son followed him, as did the crowd. Men and women from the neighbourhood came out to their porches to see the procession. Mudaliyar's wife, too, came and stood by her husband's side.

'Is that Ellappan? Wow. How handsome he's become. With a turban and a silk veshti. More like for a coronation than a cremation.'

The sound of the conch was drawn out like a long flute. Slowly, it faded away.

Mudaliyar sat down. Hearing him sit down, the cat on the chair across from him lifted her head, looked at him, lowered her head and went back to sleep.

In the midst of that sadness, Mudaliyar broke into a smile. His wife went back to the kitchen to attend to her chores.

We don't wonder at the great or look down on the lowly.[1] Singing this line, he called out to the cat, 'Hey kitty, come here.'

The cat opened her eyes.

'Come here, I said.'

The cat jumped down and approached him. He lifted her on to his lap and petted her forehead. Her eyes opened wide. Again he sang, '*We don't look down on the lowly.*'

His wife came out. 'Did you call me?'

'No, I called kitty. A life floats past by itself like a banana branch in a stream in spate. A high life or a lowly one. Everyone floats past. The poet says he won't make too much of big people nor ignore the little ones. Do you get it, kitty?'

Kitty turned over, showing her whiskers, opening her mouth, baring her sharp teeth.

'The conch was blowing. Couldn't you have got up and had a look? You were just lying down with your eyes closed. Remember how you scared Muttaiya on the day of the temple festival the year before last? . . . See, she's smiling. Very naughty.' Mudaliyar looked at her teeth.

'She's proud of herself for scaring that police superintendent. That's why she's all smiles. Shut your mouth, you little whore.' Mudaliyar's wife made kitty close her mouth. Kitty rubbed her front paw on his wife's wrist.

His wife moved away. 'Send her to me. I'll give her a little rice in warm water. She only had a glass of milk early in the morning. Hey kitty, come to me.' She stood at the door and called her. Kitty arched her back and followed her.

Mudaliyar smiled again, remembering.

Three years back, Muttaiya was transferred here as the police superintendent. He settled into a house across the street that came with the post. By the next day, he had created a dust storm. The house opposite suddenly looked deserted, without the usual hangers-on. The MLA, who used to be a frequent visitor, was not to be seen. Gopala Konar was silent—usually, you could hear him shouting at the carts carrying firewood; he'd take a cut from each one of them under the pretext of performing the temple consecration ceremony, and then auction the wood off and pocket the money. And Mamundi, the cart man, always drunk and brawling until he fell into the gutter and couldn't get out—you couldn't hear his cries and curses now, either. In the fifth street of the agraharam, even the ladies used to play cards for money. The house of Pancham Pattu Ayyar, the zamindar, in the middle of the street, was always open. After Muttaiya came, his buddies transferred their noisy parties to another district. They must have gone off to another agraharam in Tanjavur District. Muttaiya was very strict—so strict that even the Saturday and Sunday card games the government clerks used to play were stopped. The honourable weavers, both men and women, no longer relieved themselves on Station Road at dawn and dusk while smoking their cigars. People now queued up at the bus stops and the cinemas. Milk powder and sugar were sold at a fair price. The by-lanes stopped reeking of urine. Even the steps leading down to the pond were no longer slippery.

Muttaiya was the stuff of legend. They used to say he would move around in disguise. As a beggar. As a thief. As a fortune teller with his hourglass drum. As a priest. As a rake. As a merchant. All this to sniff out crime. They say that when he was posted in Tirunelveli, the neighbour's wife gave *his* wife twenty drumsticks plucked from her own garden. He thought it might be a bribe. He locked his wife up for three days and then sent her back to her parents' home for six months. He brought her back only after she fell at his feet and begged forgiveness. Are these stories true? People like to reduce good and honest men to clowns.

Mudaliyar could see Muttaiya from his window once or twice a week. Muttaiya would relax in an armchair on his porch after a late-night dinner; he'd light a cigarette and enjoy the breeze coming from the country almond and neem trees. After half an hour, he'd go inside. Mudaliyar could see the lamp burning until midnight. Maybe he was reading or writing. Or maybe he went out in disguise. On some days, Mudaliyar felt like talking to him. Finally, he gathered courage and, with kitty in his hands (she was four months old), went and stood at Muttaiya's front gate, looking at him with some hesitation. Who knows what Muttaiya was thinking? He just got up and went inside. The door was locked. The moment passed. Mudaliyar went home, blaming himself for his reticence.

One day, Muttaiya's eight-year-old son came over. He played with the kitten. Then he picked her up and took her to his house. An hour later, he brought her back. Maybe Muttaiya was out of town. Otherwise, how could the boy have had the courage to come over and play with the kitten?

That evening, after dark, Muttaiya's wife came.

She introduced herself. 'It's me, from the house across the street.'

'Come in, sit down.' Mudaliyar's wife welcomed her with excitement and the respect due to a lady of the highest station.

'Thank you . . . Is there a kitten in your house?'

'Yes, there is. Please sit down. Your boy came this afternoon and played with her. He even took her home. Please have a seat.'

'I don't have time right now. It's time for *him* to come home. From now on, if my son asks for the kitty, don't give her to him.'

'Why is that? He's just a child.'

Mudaliyar, who was listening from inside, laughed. He wondered if this, too, could be considered a bribe.

'You can give the boy whatever he asks for, but not the kitty.'

'Why so?'

'Just please don't.'

'She won't bite. She's a nice kitty.'

'It's not that. My husband doesn't like kittens.'

'He doesn't like kitties?'

'Not just dislike. If he sees a kitten, his face breaks out in hives. He can't speak. He gets the jitters and runs away.'

'What!'

'Yes. He's not afraid of a big cat. But if a kitten turns up, even if he's talking to somebody, he jumps up and runs off, his heart pounding. He even comes down with fever. When we were in Dindigul, one day, we were eating, and a kitten came in. That's all. He left the table and ran into the backyard without even washing his fingers. He might have developed this fear of kittens when he was a boy—we don't know. The fact is that he can't face a kitten. Lions, tigers, big cats—no problem. But not a kitten.' Muttaiya's wife laughed, a kindly laugh.

Mudaliyar's wife also laughed kindly.

'Today, there's a school holiday for the temple festival. The boy wanted to go to the cinema with his friends. He was pestering his father all morning, but his father said no. My husband didn't come home for lunch. The boy went on pestering me. Finally, my husband came for a late lunch. He was resting. The boy brought your kitten over. He said, "Daddy,

I brought the kitten. What do you say? Can I go to the cinema or not?" He showed him the kitten. Just that. My husband ran upstairs and closed the door. I followed after him. He asked me to phone the orderly and get him to take that little devil to the cinema. He asked me if that thing is still there. He can't even say the word "kitten". He only opened the door when he was certain that it was gone. He looked like he'd seen a ghost.'

'That's amazing.'

'Even I feel like laughing. What can I do?' said Muttaiya's wife.

She chatted for another five minutes and, repeating her warning, went home. Mudaliyar's wife sent her off with a coconut, betel leaf, pan, and kumkum, as is the custom.

As he thought it over, Mudaliyar laughed again and again. His wife joined in. Underneath that laughter, there was longing. Do children really play pranks like that? So smart? Mudaliyar's wife had hungered for a child in her belly. Mudaliyar also felt the lack. Over the years, that feeling had dried up. In the end, there was a shadow of hope. It took a whole year before the innocent heart of his wife understood that it was only menopause. Now she was fifty-three, and Mudaliyar was fifty-eight.

Whenever Mudaliyar saw Muttaiya through the window, he felt like laughing.

Today, too.

Two weeks ago, Muttaiya came back from work at midday with chest pains. He was clutching at his chest. They sent for the doctor. Muttaiya asked for water. Before they could bring it, he was gone.

What a tragedy! The older son has gone away for work. The younger boy, Ellappan, is just ten years old. How could Muttaiya have died just like that, so carelessly? All kinds of useless questions popped into Mudaliyar's mind.

Both Mudaliyar and his wife felt sorry for Muttaiyar's wife and worried about the boy.

~

'Take your bath. Food's ready,' said his wife.

When they went into the backyard, they heard the kitty's cries. They couldn't see where they were coming from. She wasn't in the bathroom. Not where they kept the firewood. Not in the toilet. It wasn't her usual 'meow, meow' but howls of terror. They looked down into the well. Kitty was trying to catch hold of the step covered with algae, but she kept slipping back into the water. She was drowning, bobbing up and down.

'Kitty!' Mudaliyar called, his voice cracking.

'Naow'—Kitty looked up. Distracted, she slipped again; struggled, sank, flailed, tried to hold on to the step. A minute passed.

'Kitty!'

Mudaliyar started crying.

'You can't just stand there crying!' They threw down a bucket attached to a rope.

'Kitty! Kitty! Catch hold of this and get into the bucket,' the wife shouted, pleaded. 'Catch it, my darling.'

The kitten duly tried four or five times but failed. Sank again.

Mudaliyar ran here and there. He couldn't keep his feet on the floor. He lowered into the well the long stick they used for plucking drumsticks. Kitty tried to hold on to it, but it was too slippery.

'What can I do, oh Goddess Rajeswari?'

He went next door with fear writ large on his face. Four or five people came running.

He didn't know what to do, and time was running out.

Shedding his shame, Mudaliyar went to the house across the street. Muttaiya's wife was lying down on her stomach after sending off her children to the funeral. Her relatives were busy cooking.

'Amma,' he said.

She turned and sat up at once.

'I didn't mean to scare your husband. The cat didn't mean to either. What does a cat know? Even if it's not on purpose, a sin is a sin. Now she's fallen into the well. She's fighting for her life.' Tears fell from his eyes.

She froze. His words didn't register in her mind.

The relatives came and asked. It took Mudaliyar two more minutes to describe things clearly.

Muttaiya's wife broke her silence. 'Call the orderly.'

The orderly came. She said, 'Call the firemen. It seems a cat has fallen into a well. Tell them to come immediately. Tell them I'm the one who's calling . . . Go, sir, the fire engine will come now.' She wanted to lie down again.

Mudaliyar ran to the telephone. The orderly made the call.

He came back home and ran into the backyard. He stood there crying. Again and again he peered into the well. He ran up and down between the gate and the backyard, looking desperately for the fire engine. Then back to the well, as if the kitty would drown if he weren't there.

'We were making fun of Muttaiya and how scared he was of kitty. That's what brought this on,' he said to his wife, his hands on his hips, raising his eyes to the sky. 'One shouldn't think ill of someone even unconsciously. Even if it doesn't happen at once, sooner or later, punishment will follow.'

Pitifully, she agreed.

'It's here!' said Mudaliyar. The two of them ran to the gate to see the fire engine.

'Sir,' Mudaliyar said, as if pleading with Yama, the god of death, 'in this house, she is our only offspring. She's son, daughter, and grandchild to us.'

One of the four firemen stood at the well, holding a rope, while another one lowered himself down.

Kitty got scared, rolled her eyes, hissed at him. She wasn't the little kitten of three years ago. She had eaten and digested enough food for all those absent children. She'd grown almost as big as a dog.

'Looks like she might scratch me,' said the fireman in the well. 'Bring me the blanket. It's under the driver's seat.'

The third fireman came running with the blanket.

As he went down, Kitty was hissing more and more, mad with fear.

Mudaliyar thought to himself, 'Wow, look how smoothly he's going down the rope.'

When he reached the algae-covered step, Kitty leaped up, growling, fell again, sank, bobbed up, sank again. Mudaliyar was crying loudly to the gods, 'Krishna! Krishna! Venkatesa!'

'Keep quiet,' said his wife.

The onlookers laughed to themselves but said: 'Poor thing.'

Five minutes passed. The fireman covered Kitty's head with the blanket and pulled her up.

'She has to breathe!'

The blanket growled.

'Let her breathe!'

'Stop it, sir. Did I catch her just to wring her neck? I came to save her. She can hold her breath for three minutes. Relax,' said the fireman, climbing out.

By the time he got out, the house was overflowing with neighbours.

Mudaliyar received the cat. He lifted up the blanket. She jumped down, passed through his legs, and ran into the front room with Mudaliyar running behind her.

She hissed at him, too, from her perch on the sofa.

'OK, OK, I'll come later,' he said. Everyone was having fun.

'At least let me dry you off,' said Mudaliyar.

Another hiss.

'OK, OK, never mind.'

The crowd dispersed. Each of the firemen got a tumbler of buttermilk and three rupees as their reward.

That's how the story of Superintendent Muttaiya and the kitty spread around, along with the other stories about him. Fortunately, when he was still alive, it didn't go beyond his own family. There was no way people could know. Mudaliyar believed that God Himself, who grants or withholds children, might have helped in this, too. He vowed to himself that he would never again let kitty scare anyone, not even a child.

Note

1. This is a line from the ancient poem *Purananuru* 192.

Debt Discharged

'Uncle, I can't believe that you let yourself be cheated like this. You say it's been three years. Couldn't you have said at least one word to me?'

'Isn't that how he protected himself? Like a scorpion stinging his prey, he told me over and over again not to let out a peep to Ratna Desigar. Otherwise, everything would be lost. I clung to that.'

'I keep on thinking about it, Uncle. I can't make peace with it. Even if you didn't, couldn't my Auntie at least have told me? Or your brother? The trust you didn't have in me you put in that rogue! Is there anyone naïve enough to believe that in this neighbourhood, a kuzhi of land costs four and a half rupees? Not even a child from here would believe it. Don't you know that even when rice was going for between three quarters of a rupee to a rupee, a kuzhi was not selling for less than five? You gave him 24,000 rupees without letting out a word. A person you had never heard of comes and tells you something, and you don't even think you should consult someone before you give him the money. It's like a child getting cheated. Auntie! Didn't it occur to you to say a word to me?' Ratna Desigar looked at his Aunt Minakshi, who was leaning against a pillar and sobbing inconsolably.

'If you were to compete with him, how could we buy a kuzhi for four and a half? That's why we didn't tell you. Like the saying goes, "If Mother gives a saree, Father gives a horse." Except for my nose ring and my earrings, I gave everything I had on me.' She choked up and, unable to control her crying, went inside.

Ratna Desigar was stunned. Tears flowed from the eyes of Sundara Desigar, who was lying on a cot.

'Ratnam, I sold the lands. I took all the money from the bank. All of it. I gave him every jewel and ornament my wife had on her. She had jewels worth more than 4,000 rupees. I threw it all away.

Only today did she speak to anybody about it. After all, she had to tell someone. She hasn't told any living creature except you. She couldn't hold it in any more. Look, how many people I have embittered. Even if we leave my wife out of this, there's my brother, his wife, his children—without consulting anybody, I took full advantage of being the elder and brought everything to ruin. But not a single soul in this family has said a word. At least in that way, I am lucky. But I will be answerable to God, right? I think about it endlessly. How could a man be so stupid? I just can't understand how I could have handed over tons of money. Did he cast a spell on me? Or did that crook knock out my common sense and drag me into the street? I don't understand it.' Sundara Desigar slumped in a daze.

Ratna Desigar took the letters that were lying there in a bunch and read them one by one. Ramadas Nayudu's name was not even in one of them. 'I got the money. Salutations. We'll make arrangements to register the documents soon.' 'I received the money. Within a week or two we'll see to the documents.' Blandly, without mentioning the sum, the letters ended with, 'Yours, Kandasamy.' Every letter had 'Mylapore' written at the top. No address. Who is that Kandasamy? Ratna Desigar even doubted that there was such a person. Only God knows who he is. Even He may not know. What if he had made up that guy in the first place? Only Ramadas could tell. Ramadas has already given us the slip. For the last two months, he's been keeping his head down. If you ask his wife, you won't get anything from her except 'I don't know.'

Ratna Desigar kept looking at the thirty or thirty-two letters. There was no trace of the 24,000 that he had taken. The letters only use the word 'money'. Couldn't there be even one letter that said, 'I got the money from Ramadas Nayudu'? The wretched law needs evidence. What can you say to a law that says you are a murderer only if there's a witness on hand? Ratna Desigar was amazed at how cleverly he had deceived his uncle.

Ramadas, who used to come every day like a sentry at the door, had disappeared for two months. Sundara Desigar kept looking for him. 'The money's gone. Everything is lost.' He was so shaken that he fell ill and took to bed. If he doesn't get the money back, there's little chance that he'll survive. Ratna Desigar was at a loss.

For a while, neither of them spoke. At last Ratna Desigar said, 'Uncle, we need to lodge a complaint with the police and get a warrant issued against him. Don't worry too much. I'll take care of it. If you had told me a bit earlier, we wouldn't have reached this point. There's no point in going over it all again. Don't lose heart.'

'Lose heart? I don't need much—I don't even care that much about my property. If my property makes someone else happy and content, I'm satisfied. But does all this property belong to me? There's my brother. He has a big family. He never objects to anything I say. If I think about him, I can't get over it.'

'Stop thinking about it all the time. Stop hurting yourself. It's all due to bad times. We have no control over things.'

'OK. You've been my right hand all along. God has punished me enough for not trusting you. I feel awkward even talking to you.'

'Don't say such things. It's a bad time for us. What could we do? I'll take my leave.'

'OK.'

Sundara Desigar sat looking into the void. It was the baffling hour of dusk. From a distance, the imperious ringing of the church bell. A single star bursting over the courtyard. When it came to his personal affairs, all his learning, wisdom, and knowledge had become worthless. That surprised him.

He's sixty years old. An expert in Saiva Siddhanta. When he starts singing *Tevaram*, his voice carries over three octaves with ease, without any false notes, resonant as a finely tuned tambura. There is a steady stream of people seeking his advice about disputes among brothers, quarrels between husband and wife, partitioning property, and fixing auspicious occasions. He has earned respect and praise as an elder of the community, never swerving from what is right. He is also a man of property. This is the man Ramadas Nayudu chose to deceive.

Sundara Desigar never had a close friendship with Ramadas Nayudu. He knows all five or six thousand people in Appamangalam. They all greet him as an elder of the village. Ramadas was one in that great crowd.

For some unknown reason, out of the blue, Ramadas Nayudu fastened on to him.

Just like now, one evening, at the baffling hour of dusk. Sundara Desigar was sitting on his pyol, savouring the fragrance of cloves, silently going over a raga in his mind. Ramadas was passing by. Sundara Desigar hadn't seen him for some time.

'How are you, Ramadas? I haven't seen you.'

'Why would I disappear?' Ramadas slipped off his sandals at the door, came in and sat down.

'You're well?'

'Yes.'

'How is casuarina timber selling?'

'Casuarina? It's been a year since I closed my shop.'

'Closed your shop? I didn't know. Why?'

'No business. A huge effort yielding nothing.'

'You're not somebody who can just sit around! Now that you've closed the shop, what are you doing?'

'I'm doing some kind of brokerage. I'm in real estate. Looking for deals.'

'Limited effort, big return.'

'It's not that big. Enough for food.'

'If you get four deals in a year, that's enough.'

'That's true.'

'Even if you put yourself out for one month, you'll be able to take it easy for eleven months.'

'That's right.'

'Are you taking in hundreds or thousands?'

'Would I be sitting here if I were raking in thousands? If I got money like that, I'd have bought four houses by now. At the moment, there's something coming up. I don't know who will luck out. If he buys, something big may come my way. Now is the moment—like finding a treasure. We don't know who is out there.'

'Land or a house?'

'It's land, sir. Very precious. Two yields per year. One lot is about 15 acres. The first crop, from June to September, will be 20 kalams, and the second crop, from October to December, will also be 20 kalams. Even in a drought, the two yields together won't be less than 35.'

'Where is the site?'

'Here, in Punganceri.'

'Punganceri? No wonder. The yield can be twenty or even thirty. What's the price?'

'Four and a half.'

'Ah!'

Desigar was taken aback.

'How can that be, in Punganceri? Four and a half!'

'Not so loud. It will ruin everything.'

Desigar lowered his voice.

'You must be joking. In that area, land goes for nothing less than fifteen.'

'We shouldn't be talking about this, sitting here outside. If we go inside, I'll tell you.'

'Fine, come inside.' Desigar got up and went in. Ramadas's conscience rose up for a moment, a cobra spreading its hood. He beat it back down and gave himself over to the game. He followed Desigar inside. Desigar offered him a chair.

'It's OK,' said Ramadas, and sat down on the floor.

'Ramadas, what kind of riddle is this? Are you out of your mind? I don't understand anything.'

'Right, it's almost beyond belief. But the lucky person will believe it.'

'Is it for real? Four and a half!' Desigar asked innocently, amazed.

'Yes. The owner works in a company in Madras. The lessee keeps dodging him. The owner is eager to settle down in the city. You could say he's given to new-fangled trends. It's an inherited property. His father also had a job in Madras. He passed away. The present owner was born in the city and grew up there. He knows nothing of life in the village. He was afraid a long-term tenant might claim ownership, so he kept changing the lease from one person to another. That's why he's come to the village four or five times. Apart from that, he doesn't know the village. He can't even find his field unless someone shows it to him. He can't find someone he could rely on to send him paddy or cash. How could he find someone if he has no real feeling for the village? He just wants to be in the city. He's eager to sell. That's the story. I visited him last week. He told me. When I asked him how much, he said four and a half. And me, I couldn't believe it. Just by listening to him talk, I could see he knows nothing about the village. He must be hard-pressed for money, some twenty or twenty-five thousand. On a whim, he said four and a half. I thought I would grab it myself, fast, without anybody knowing. But how could I come up with twenty thousand? Who would trust me and give me that much money? It's not practical.

So I said to myself, OK, it's my fate to be content with a thousand or two. All I want, since I can't get it myself, is that I should be able to close the deal for someone I care about. But there's no person like that I can trust. When I tell you that in Punganceri land goes for four and half, it's like saying that a person who wears a loincloth in the land of the naked is crazy. Will anybody believe that kind of thing? Meanwhile, there's a vulture from this place hovering around.'

'Who's that?'

'It's someone you know. Ratna Desigar. Within a week, he's already gone to Madras twice. I saw him on the road to Punganceri the day before yesterday. "What are you doing?" I asked. "I just came to feel the breeze." Is there no breeze in our village? He was putting me on. I nodded and went away.'

'So Ratnam is on to this? Then he'll certainly clinch it.'

'Will he? He's Ratnam, and I'm Ramadas. My *Ra* is longer than his.'

'That's okay, but how will you get around him?'

'An advance of three thousand rupees will nail it.'

'Can you do it?'

'If I had the money, for sure.'

'How much?'

'Three thousand will do.'

'OK, don't worry. Come tomorrow afternoon at 4.'

'Who for?'

'For someone here.'

'Tell me who.'

'Assume it's for me.'

'Then it's fine. It's like a mango falling into a bowl of milk. That's what I was hoping. But don't let word get out. Be careful.'

'In these matters, how can we not be careful?'

'I just said it out of my own nervousness.'

'Don't worry. Come tomorrow at 4.'

The next day, Desigar withdrew two thousand rupees that he had kept in the bank for an emergency. He took another thousand on a promissory note from Vaittiyanada Pillai, who ran a hardware shop. He finished all this before lunch. At 4, Ramadas took the three thousand.

Greetings . . . The money arrived. . . . I'll make arrangements for registration soon. The rest in person.—Ra. Kandasamy.

That evening at dusk, Ramadas came. He had also received a letter. He showed it to Sundara Desigar.

Two days later, a letter arrived for Ramadas from Mylapore.

> *. . . The money arrived. I have written to Desigar. We'll make arrangements for registration soon. Show Desigar the land.*—Ra. Kandasamy.

'Why see the land? Your word is enough,' said Desigar.

'That's not right. It's always good to have a look at the land. You can't do anything without having a look. What if you're not satisfied later?'

'OK, if you want to. When shall we go?'

'I'm ready whenever you come.'

'Shall we go on Thursday?'

'It's best if we go before dawn or at dusk. It's good to keep it under wraps until it's signed and sealed.'

'All right. I'll come at dawn on Thursday.'

On Thursday, before the darkness lifted, Desigar harnessed his cart and drove himself. At the end of the village, Ramadas was waiting; he climbed into the cart and took the reins. Desigar skipped his morning bath for the first time in forty years.

It was four miles to Punganceri. Dawn was breaking as they reached it. There was a cool morning breeze. The drongo had woken up before the village and was now waking it up. The silence of the dawn, the cool breeze, and the excitement he felt—all these made up for the missed morning bath.

'Look who's standing there,' said Ramadas as he stopped the cart.

'Who?' asked Desigar.

'He's the lessee. Let's get off here. We'll untie the bullocks here. The land is nearby. We can come back in a few minutes. We can tie the bullocks to a tree.'

'OK.'

Those two and a half veli were four fields away. The three of them walked along the bund.

Ramadas said, 'I know this man well. Hello, there. From now on, this gentleman is going to be the new owner of the land.'

'Obviously.'

Desigar stood under the acacia tree and looked around. The lush, dark green paddy was rolling like waves in the morning breeze.

'It's truly a Kaveri crop. Look how elegant the paddy looks, and how alive! What would be the average yield?'

'The first crop—no less than eighteen to twenty. The second crop won't be under sixteen or seventeen.'

'And the lease?'

'Twenty-five.'

'That's a bit high.'

'So you say. The owner thinks it's very low. The owner wants me to pay the land tax as well. It's unheard of. What lessee ever pays the land tax? That's a problem. What can you say to someone who asks you on what tree paddy grows? Someone who has no idea about the worth of the man who works the soil, or about our practices and customs. He doesn't know what he's asking.'

'You don't need to worry about this any more, my friend. You'll soon get to know what kind of a man the new owner is.'

'The land looks good. And the lessee says the yield, too, is good,' said Desigar with a surge of happiness within as he looked at the dark green crop.

'This lessee is a hard worker. He won't shirk the job just because it's a lease,' said Ramadasu.

'Why shirk? The Earth Goddess is just waiting to give. If you feed her well, she'll repay you handsomely. There's treasure just lying here. Shouldn't we make at least the little effort that is required? One would have to be foolish to shirk the task.'

'So you say, young man. If everyone were like you, would feeding the people in this country be a headache for the government? We're just lazy. We expect that rice will fall into our mouth just like that without any effort. That's why this country is struggling,' said Desigar, still staring at the land.

'Well . . . I work hard without grudging it. I care for the land, give it all it needs, like for my own child. The lease should stay with me; it's God's will.'

'Don't worry, my friend. If you work hard, why would I change the lease to someone else?'

'You don't have to say any more. He knows,' said Ramadas.

After a while, the three of them went back to the road.

The cart set off. As they entered the village, Ramadas handed over the reins to Desigar and said, 'Don't take it amiss if I repeat myself. Don't let anybody know about this. If Ratna Desigar gets wind of it, everything is lost.' With this warning, Ramadas climbed down.

'Do you think I'm crazy? Don't worry about that,' Desigar reassured him.

The cart was gone. Ramadas, standing on the bank of the irrigation canal, took out a penknife and cut off a small twig from the acacia tree to chew on. He felt a twinge of pity for Desigar in his heart. But no qualms. 'The poor guy is so trusting.' He felt sorry.

The two and a half veli that Desigar saw actually belonged to the Konkanesar temple in Punganceri. The 'lessee' was a cattle broker in Tanjavur. He collected his fee of ten rupees and took the next bus to Tanjavur after playing his part.

'The damned fellow, so unlucky! So easily deceived. Even now, if he could see through the whole drama, he'd get away.' For an instant, Ramadas wished his own defeat. Desigar's childlike innocence had brought him to this point. Ramadas found it difficult to shrug off these thoughts.

It took Desigar a long time to fall asleep that night. In his mind, he saw that stretch of two and a half velis becoming his, and his heart pounded with joy.

Ramadas came every day without fail and chatted with him for half an hour. After fifteen days, he asked for eight thousand. Immediately, Desigar sold off twelve mas[1] of family property, wetland and dry land, at the high price of fifteen rupees a kuzhi, collected the cash and handed over eight thousand rupees to Ramadas. Soon, a letter arrived from Mylapore. Desigar paid off his debt to Vaittiyanada Pillai.

A month passed. The person from Mylapore was still busy. But Ramadas brought Desigar four cartloads of first-grade paddy and sacks of hay for the cows and buffaloes.

Four months passed. Another thousand, another four thousand went to Ramadas, followed by letters. After the second crop, another four cartloads of paddy arrived. Desigar had no worries about food. His first great love was for Padiri mangoes from Mayavaram. Four or five basketfuls arrived. His second great love was for tender mango from the Madurai hills. Ramadas took great care to satisfy all his private longings.

'You're a person who knows how to do things just right,' said Desigar one day. For Ramadas, this pat on the back was like a pat on his wounded conscience. The sting became bearable. He recovered thickly.

The cash from the sale of the land evaporated entirely. Still, the two and a half velis of land that he was hoping to get by selling twelve ma was tantalizingly close but not within his grasp.

Desigar was confused.

Ramadas kept asking for money the way you have to feed the fire in a brick kiln. Desigar thought it was better to give more in order to recover what he had already given. Minakshiyammal's bangles, choker, three-strand chain, and the heirloom pendant she wore—one by one, they all turned into currency. Two years went by. The Mylapore man kept writing letters and making excuses.

Another six months went by. There was no need to worry about food. There was plenty of paddy in the house. Where did it come from?

Suddenly Ramadas stopped coming.

Desigar lost his nerve. He got fever. He panicked. He took to bed. Ratna Desigar, his nephew once removed, came from the next village to see him. 'Ratnam, do you know this Ramadas?' Desigar asked him, casually.

'I know him.'

'What sort of a guy is he?'

'Why, have you lent him any money?'

'Why are you asking?'

'Otherwise, why would anyone inquire about him? If you gave him a hundred or two hundred, you can forget about it. Don't give him any more.'

Desigar went into shock. In the course of an hour, he spit it all out.

Ratna Desigar felt as if he'd been struck a hard blow. Anonymous letters, foolishness—it all unnerved him. He felt lost.

They lodged a complaint with the police. The next day, the whole village was buzzing. People came in droves to comfort him. They also found it amusing. Life was somehow still clinging to his body. Kannusamy Pillai, chairman of the Panchayat Board, Dr Kuppusamy, Suppatta, and four or five others were at his bedside.

'These days, a father doesn't trust his son. A wife, children, brothers—no one is trusted. And you trusted a riff-raff like him?'

'That damned fellow cheated you, of all people! He should be tortured to death inch by inch.'

'You know how lavishly he would eat? Every day, he helped himself to two jangiris or two halwahs and gulped down "degree coffee", the swine.'

'Fresh dhotis and well-ironed shirts . . . For New Moon day, he took his wife to Vedaranyam, and to Ramesvaram for Sivaratri.'

Shock, hatred, and affection were dancing in disorder before Desigar's eyes.

'You may wonder why I say these words. I have some satisfaction when I see a person get so much happiness with my money. Kannusamy Pillai, it seems you don't agree with what I'm saying. When all of you are so stirred up, my words sound hypocritical, like the cat wearing prayer beads in the story. It's not just sour grapes. It truly gives me satisfaction. So what if that money is gone? My Nataraja, my Sabhapati Peruman, will give me some other money. That's for sure. At first, I was completely shattered because everything was lost. But when I thought it over, it seemed like it didn't matter. I'm not worried now. My money will definitely come back.'

'So can we let that scoundrel off the hook?'

'That's not what I'm saying. Anyone who commits fraud must be punished. I want the government to punish him. What I said is just a thought that came to my mind.'

In fact, at heart everyone wanted to drink Ramadas's blood.

Twenty days later, Ramadas was caught near Chidambaram. They dragged him away in handcuffs.

His face put on a look of surprise. 'What money? Me take money from Desigar? What sort of riddle is this?' Then they inserted needles under his fingernails. His whole back swelled up, and his face, too, was swollen.

He hadn't anticipated this stage. Being beaten up like a dog was not part of the plan. He came out on bail.

The case was heard in court. He lied, swore an oath that he didn't write the letters. When he came out of the courtroom that day, Kannusamy Pillai spat at him.

His last five hundred or thousand rupees got spent.

~

One day, Ramadas fell sick with a headache. A headache that wouldn't go away. It got worse. He developed a fever. His body began to wither away like a crop of okra eaten up by pests. He was bedridden. He had no money to buy medicine. His conscience, beaten down again and again, with its tail wrapped around it, now flared up, blazing brightly. He didn't have the strength of mind to beat it back down. There was no sign he would recover. It was not yet three weeks. He was reduced to counting the minutes, to dying that day or the next.

It was eight in the morning.

'Warm water, please,' said Ramadas.

'He's here,' she said, with alarm in her voice.

'Who?'

'Desigar.'

'Ratna Desigar?'

'No, it's our Desigar.'

'Oh.'

Before he closed his mouth, Sundara Desigar came in. He looked around. The stench of tattered, dirty clothes, of the body wasting away, turned his stomach. Ramadas's wife couldn't grasp what was happening. She pointed to a chair and asked him to sit down.

'Ramadas, I heard that you're ill. Seriously ill. I just wanted to see you. Not only that. I have something important to say.'

Ramadas was lying on a coir cot. He lacked the strength even to raise himself to lean against a pillow.

'Ramadas, I don't think I've ever seen a man as smart as you. In this world, people slog to find happiness. Very few achieve it as easily as you. But finally you were caught. If I win, you'll be punished. But I don't believe I will win. You cheated me so skilfully. But if you do win the case, I think there will be no one as unfortunate as you. Anyone who does wrong, anyone who commits a crime, has to atone for it by suffering intensely in both mind and body. If he doesn't, the sin will gnaw at him. So when I heard about your condition, I came running. Who cares who wins the case? Your life is ebbing away. I rushed here because I was afraid you wouldn't find your way. Our scriptures say that one mustn't die without repaying one's debts. You have to pay off your debt now, and I have to declare, wholeheartedly, that you owe me nothing. That's why I'm here. With my money, you paid off your earlier debts. You enjoyed your life. I heard all about it. I was really happy. But you must not go without clearing the debt. I checked with your neighbours. They said you have no money to even pay the doctor. So I ask only one thing of you. Give me whatever you have, it will do. Even if it is only five rupees, or one rupee. I will happily accept it, and I'll swear by the holy *Tevaram*, by the goddess who protects the earth, that you have paid off the debt. What do you say? That's why I came.' Desigar paused, waiting for a reply.

It took Ramadas a little while to take all this in. He was terrified. He thought his life, writhing with pain, had fallen into the fire.

'I'm telling you this honestly. Whatever you give will be enough. I'll say, with all my heart, that some twenty thousand have been paid, and I'll go away.'

Sundara Desigar heard someone crying. He turned to look. Ramadas's wife, trembling all over, barely controlling her sobbing, approached Ramadas. She took his shrunken, withered right hand and put something in it; then she pulled the hand towards Desigar.

Sundara Desigar took the hand and took the two-anna coin that was in it.

'Amma, why are you still crying? Be at peace. My debt has been released. I say it with Goddess Parasakti as my witness. Your husband has fully cleared the debt. Don't worry any more. He, too, can rest. I'll take my leave.' Sundara Desigar left.

Note

1. One hundred kuzhis equal one ma. Twenty mas make a veli (6.6 acres).

The Music Lesson

Everyone made fun of Mallikai. He wasn't sure everyone was doing it, but that's how it seemed to him. The first one who asked about it was certainly making fun of him and went away laughing. That's why Malli thought that anyone who asked was teasing him.

In the morning, as usual, he bathed in the river, finished his prayers and puja, had his dosai and coffee, and came to sit on the pyol. It was about 8.30. The speaker attached to the radio on the co-op at the far end of the village had fallen silent. Sunlight was starting to brighten the whole street, and it was getting hotter. The children had gone to school in the next village. The street was deserted. Suddenly, the servant from Subbukkutti's house rode through the street carrying a cartload of paddy saplings. After that, the noise ceased. Seven or eight houses away, Racu had spread out a huge bulrush mat, with rocks placed at the corners so they wouldn't curl up, and was smoothing out heaps of dried coconuts that he had brought from inside the house, for the oil press.

Then Balan, passing by, looked at Malli sitting on the pyol and asked, 'So, Malli?'

'Yes, Uncle?'

'I heard something.'

'What?'

'It seems you said you're going to teach Kuppandi music.' Balan laughed, his bare chest bobbing up and down.

'Yes.'

'What do you mean, "yes"?' asked Balan, laughing some more, surprise laced with sarcasm.

'Why are you laughing?'

'Why are you doing that?' Another question.

'He has a good voice. Intuitive understanding. I think he'll turn out well,' said Malli.

'So . . . you think he, of all persons, can be taught?'

'Why, Uncle? What's wrong with teaching him?'

Balan looked at Malli as if he were taken aback. 'What can I say when you ask why?' He looked east and west down the street, laughing all the while. 'OK, but where will he sit while you're teaching him?'

Malli hadn't expected this question. Indeed, where will Kuppandi sit? He was shocked that he hadn't thought about it.

'Tell me,' Balan urged him.

'I still haven't thought about it, Uncle,' said Malli.

'You didn't think about it?' he cackled.

For a moment, Malli cringed. He had been so foolish. Done something so laughable, and now he was unable to answer a legitimate question.

'You're not thinking of bringing him inside the house, are you?' said Balan.

'What are you saying, Uncle?' Malli was stunned.

'The way things are going, is there anything wrong in what I asked?'

'How come you asked such a question? Did you think I would take him inside and teach him there?' Malli said, aggrieved. Balan, without hearing him out, started to move off, still laughing. 'They've let them into the temple; they've let them into the Brahmin street; and now, if you're willing, you can let them into your house, just like Gandhi. It has to happen. Who knows? Nobody can stop anything any more. Enjoy yourself.' He untucked the end of his dhoti and went down into the street, as if he had something much more important than this to do, as if someone he was expecting was coming; shielding his eyes from the heat, he walked off, looking at the end of the street. Balan was the most important among the three elders of the village. Though he didn't have much property, he had earned status because of his age and the way he spoke. People would listen to him.

Malli was squirming, still thinking about those questions, not yet recovered from the shock of his own foolishness.

Within a few minutes, Sitaraman, a man of property, with a stud in his ear and a huge body, was passing by in the street. 'Uncle, what's that I've heard? You're going to teach Kuppandi music?' he said, standing in the street, as if to say, 'Tell me quickly, I'm in a hurry.'

'Yes. He has a good voice. Seems intelligent.'

'By all means—who can say who has what these days? Whoever it may be, it's a fine thing to give knowledge.' Sitaraman moved on. He didn't say it innocently; he spoke with a slightly wicked smile.

Later, so many people asked this same question, as if they had been coached! Venkataraman, Ramaiya, Dandapani with his elephantiasis, Sami Shastri, the village accountant—all of them in their forties or fifties. Even Vali, Gopali, Manjan, who were in their twenties, would not leave him in peace. Vali had no cunning. But there was curiosity in his voice, as if he meant to say, 'Would anyone do such a wrong thing?' And as for Gopali, that bug—he laughed hard when he asked. For a long time, he'd been suffering from fits. He was skinny as a straw. Except for eating and falling sick with fever, he couldn't do anything. And even this fellow mocked him!

Pattamaniyam, the village headman, didn't ask anything. He walked by without a word. Not that he wouldn't have known. But he walked by as if to say, 'Why speak of such foolishness?'

As if the men were not enough, three old women also asked the question. Grandma Vembu was half insane. She didn't have anyone. No way to get food. She too asked with a laugh.

Malli thought he couldn't take any more of this. He went inside and sat down on the swing. His wife had gone to bathe in the river. The swing was creaking.

What to do now?

How had the news spread through the entire village? Even if it did, why does each and every person have to come and ask about it or make fun of him?

And why do I feel an inexplicable pity and fear?

The day before yesterday morning, Malli had gone to pick flowers in the backyard of the choultry[1] next to the Pillaiyar temple. He shook the coral jasmine plant and, as he gathered up the fallen flowers and put them in his kudalai basket, he started humming a raga—Dhanyasi, wasn't it? Whenever he sees the red stem of the coral jasmine flower, he feels like singing Dhanyasi. He wondered about the connection.

At that very moment, he heard a voice from somewhere, picking up the note he was singing. Whatever phrase he sang, that voice repeated it, added something, and made it even more beautiful. Malli stopped singing and listened carefully. What a voice! What a voice! He'd only heard one voice like that.

In the days when his family was sharing a house in Georgetown in Madras with eleven other families, with the kitchen at the back and the bedroom upstairs, at 1.00 or 2.00 in the night, a young fellow passed by, singing. He was a *motor car cleaner* in a garage. He sang exactly like Kittappa, Rajaratnam, and Bhagavatar—all the ragas in the dramas and the cinema songs. His voice had a pleasant tinge of gruffness—an enviable clarity, vibrato, timbre. That was when Malli understood that native genius is one thing and virtuosity another. Ninety-nine per cent of those who were in the front line of concerts or in the music world in general were there because of their practice. He somehow felt that they weren't born to sing. After that, despite listening to many discussions and hearing many concerts, that thought, which had struck him like lightning, never went away. It became an obsession. The voice he heard now was like that—intoxication embodied.

It was four or five years since Malli had settled in this village. How come he didn't know who this was? He picked up the basket and walked in the direction of the voice. He left the choultry backyard, crossed the canal, and reached the road. The voice was getting closer. It was coming from a clump of bamboo. As he came near, he heard it from amidst the thorns of the bamboo. A head appeared, with a cloth turban.

'Who's that singing?' Malli asked.

A body came into view. Kuppandi!

'Aren't you Michael's son?'

'Yes, sir.'

'Was that you singing?'

'Just like that, Sami.' Shyly, he turned his face away. 'Yes, sir. Just like that. Don't think anything of it. I won't do it again.' He said all this as if he were standing on a thorn amidst the thorns; as if to say, pleading, 'I won't sing any more. Please be kind and go away.'

'Who taught you all this?'

'Nothing like that, sir.'

'You have a fabulous voice! You just picked it up by yourself? Nobody taught you?'

'Please leave me alone, sir,' he said, squirming with shyness.

'Where did you hear all this?'

'It's the nagaswaram, sir.'

'And then?'

'Oh no, sir. I have work. This fence has to go up by evening.'

'Don't make a fuss, just tell me. Did you hear the nagaswaram in the temple festival?'

'Yes, sir.' There was a weariness in his voice.

'Where else?'

'Please let me be.'

'Are you going to tell me or not?'

'Cinema, Terukkuttu. Enough. You can leave me now.'

'You didn't study with anyone?'

'I told you, no one.'

'Do you know what it would be like if you learnt music properly? Do you know how well you sing? Shouldn't you be taking lessons?'

'Aiyaiyo!'

'I'm going to teach you myself.'

'I have work to do.'

'I've also put everything aside and am sitting here in this village of idiots. I'm definitely going to teach you. Songs, rhythms, everything. Afterwards, you can show your priest how you sing. Then you'll see. He'll invite you to sing inside the church on Sunday. Next year . . .'

'What are you saying, sir?'

'That's the kind of talent you have! If you can be trained to sing well, Christ will be pleased with you, won't he? You won't have to stand outside the fence. You'll be singing inside the church, right next to the priest. He'll have you next to him and tell you to sing. Look, today is Tuesday, isn't it? Come to my house on Friday morning. You don't have to pay me anything. Just bring a coconut and a couple of bananas. You have to say a prayer and pay respect to your teacher before you begin. It's only for that. You don't even have to cut grass for my cows. I'm going to teach you for free. What do you say? Just say you'll come. God has given you talent, hasn't he? It's a shame not to develop it and use it well. Why did God give you this gift? So you can waste your time with the thorns and sing any which way?'

Malli bombarded him from all sides. He cajoled, he threatened, he pleaded.

'What is it you want me to do?' Kuppandi said at last.

'You have to come to my house on Friday. Then every day, in the morning, you have to learn. See what happens in two years.'

'All right.'

'Afterwards, you won't have to be stitching these thorns. You'll be a big musician, wearing shirt and studs like a Bhagavatar. You'll be giving concerts like the Ammapettai musicians. I promise you . . .'

'All right, sir.'

I got him.

'I'll be waiting at dawn on Friday. If you don't turn up, I won't leave you alone.'

'I told you I'll come.'

At that moment, Malli felt like burning up the whole village. Such a bunch of ignoramuses. Don't they have anything besides cattle, dung, seeds, paddy, fertilizer, urea, sulphate, cattle sheds, water gates?

Malli was full of excitement. What a voice! What a talent! Once I teach you, once I inscribe all of it on your brain, you'll sing so splendidly . . .

He choked up.

Ever since he had come to the village four years ago, there'd been nothing but depression and weariness. Who is there to ask him to sing? Was it any better before that? He had gone to Madras wanting to be a great musician. As if the timing were bad, he had to beg to get even ten concerts. He ended up eking out a living by giving music lessons. Instead of falling at the feet of the high and mighty, it was more effective to fall at the feet of the lowly. They understand our suffering. But in the end, even that was of little use. Imagine how lucky you are if you are able to earn enough for you and your wife in Madras! When there's a village where you can live your life without having to pay rent or buy rice, milk, buttermilk, and vegetables, who needs Madras or Bombay? When you are reduced to singing for your supper, a remote village where you don't have to sing for food is better than heaven.

One day, like a woman who has lost her husband and gone back to the village, Malli packed up four sacks of utensils, some old mattresses, a wooden bureau and two chairs that he had bought from his earnings in Madras, a clock, the sruti box, and a few books on music and spiritual things; he went home. For two or three years, he sat every day and sang for himself. Gradually, that too dwindled away. He reached the point where it seemed to be enough if he went to the neighbouring villages to sing bhajans at Radha kalyanam and Ekadasi.[2] Like in the saying, 'The more you sing, the better you sing; the more you clam up, the sicker you get,' even on those occasions, he found his voice faltering. In all of Madras, with its two million people, he had only three friends who said he sang with clarity and precision. By that count, how many could he find in this village that didn't even have two hundred people? No one, no one, no one.

Three years ago, a lone disciple turned up. A young boy who had studied Sanskrit. A good voice. But he didn't have the patience to study for even six months. He went off to Madras to earn money. They said he was doing there what Malli had done in his early days. He went from place to place, grovelling before the secretaries of the music clubs, begging them to arrange for him to give discourses on the Puranas; during the performance, he would sing the praises of the honoured guests and pass a plate around . . .

How was it that for so long I had no idea that a person like Kuppandi exists!

But Balan's laughter, and the laughter of the others, and even the old women making faces—what can you say about all that?

The swing is squeaking. You want to keep on listening to it. His wife returned. She'd cooked his meal, and she served it to him. While serving, she said, 'They say that Kuppandi is going to be taught music?'

'Yes.'

'Valamba Granny asked me at the ghat.'

'How did she ask?'

'"Tell me, what's all this big city fashion? I hear that your husband is going to teach him right inside the house." I said I don't know anything, Granny. you should ask my husband.'

'Why didn't you ask her who told her?'

'I only heard about it there, at the ghat—about the lessons.' She poked at him, hinting at the distance between them.

That was what was left of their love. There was another reason for his depression. She was angry that he couldn't give her a child. He had the same complaint about her.

He didn't go back to the pyol after his meal. He shut himself up inside. He had a habit of going to the Pillaiyar temple. Now that also scared him. He confined himself to the swing. Only after it was dark did he step out to the temple. And even then, through the backyard. After worshiping the god, he thought: Why not go to the ceri and tell Kuppandi not to come tomorrow? He would have to go through the fields, walking on the bunds. Through the threshing floor. Half the way, the path was good. But he might come across someone on the threshing floor . . . That question again. Could he go the whole way along the bunds? . . . But what's going on? Who is going to stop me? Am I a coward?

Malli went home.

He ate his dinner and lay down. It was a little stuffy inside. He didn't go outside, as was his habit. Fear was churning his stomach. He went to lie down on the squeaky swing. There was a little breeze.

But the fear? It didn't go away. People talk about conscience. Is this it? He tried to figure out what conscience means. He understood that his worry was not related to his conscience. But the fear? . . . Why is it still gnawing at me? Everyone is ganging up on me and holding me down. Balan, Subbukkutti, Sitaraman, the karnam[3]—all of them control the village. 'You're ruining us!' Balan Uncle comes along to beat him, waving his arms and rolling his eyes.

'What is this? What is this?'

As if someone had pushed him. But there was no one. His wife was shaking him awake.

'What's this shouting, almost howling? Was it a dream or what?'

With the dream, he lost his sleep. He fell asleep only after 1.00.

'Isn't it time to get up?' His wife woke him. 'Kuppandi is calling you from the backyard.'

Malli got up. Quickly, he went to the backyard. Kuppandi was standing beside the cattle shed with coconut and bananas in his hands.

'Greetings to you, sir.'

'So you're here—I'll be back in a minute.' Malli brushed his teeth and came back with the sruti box.

'Put down the coconut and the bananas and say a prayer.'

He fell full length to the ground. Malli sat down on a dry patch beside the well and removed the cloth cover from the sruti box.

'Sit there—right there, next to the curry leaf plant.'

Kuppandi sat down, folding his feet. There was a distance of at least forty feet between the two men. Some seven or eight basil plants as well. Also an Andi Mandarai shrub.

'Repeat after me. First, I'll sing *sa pa sa*. Listen to it once. Afterwards, I'll sing them one by one. Then you sing—*sa pa s*a—OK? Sing now. *Sa . . .*'

'*Sa*.'

Wow. What a voice!

Sa ri ga ma pa dha ni sa, sa ni dha pa ma ga ri sa
Sa ri ga ma sa ri ga ma sa ri ga ma pa dha ni sa
Sa ni dha pa sa ni dha pa sa ni dha pa ma ga ri sa

First tempo, second tempo, third tempo . . . What a talent this fellow has! What speed? How pleasing to the ear! He's a devil of a singer.

Kuppandi had forgotten to close the opening in the fence. Some twenty people, from both the non-Brahmin street and the ceri. Along the fence of the neighbouring houses, the VIPs from the agraharam. Middle-aged people, urchins . . . Balan, Subbukkutti, the karnam, Sitaraman!

Balan laughs. The karnam laughs. Half the kids seem confused. The other half laugh without knowing why.

The people from the non-Brahmin street looked at the forty feet between Malli and Kuppandi and laughed.

Malli felt as if a haystack was burning in his stomach. The first lesson came to an end.

'*Sa pa sa*.'

'*Sa pa sa*.'[4]

'That will do for today. Come back tomorrow morning, just like today.'

Kuppandi got up and left. The crowd from the non-Brahmin street and the ceri went with him.

From the other side of the fence, Balan said, 'Bravo, Malli. You carried it off well.'

The karnam said, 'You managed to taste the gruel without wetting your moustache.'[5]

Hearing this, Sitaraman laughed hard, his chest and belly shaking. He was a big man, in more ways than one. So all the others laughed along with him. The kids and the grown-ups from the neighbour's backyard joined in at once.

Malli stood up and looked at them for a while.

'Why the hell are you laughing?'

Sitaraman mimicked him: 'Why the hell are you laughing?' Again, a burst of laughter.

'What the fuck . . .' Malli started to say. Without completing the curse, he said, 'Just wait. Tomorrow I'll have him inside my house for the lesson, damn you fools.' He picked up the sruti box and threw it at them. It hit the fence, and a thorn pierced the bellows. Feeling foolish, Malli went to pick it up. Quickly he took it, slammed the back door to the house, bolted it, went inside, and removed the thorn.

His wife, standing behind the closed door, raised her hands to the sky and let out a curse. 'Go to hell, all of you.'

'Leave them alone. Only dogs bark. Why bark with them? Come inside. I need some glue,' Malli shouted.

Fear, loneliness, and indifference suddenly took hold of him. His hand trembled, as if he had fever.

He lay down on the swing, hands clenched on the chain.

Notes

1. A choultry or cattiram is a common space where pilgrims or travellers can rest and get food and water.
2. The ritual celebrating the wedding of Radha and Krishna involves singing bhajans. Ekadasi is the eleventh day of each lunar fortnight, an auspicious moment.
3. The village accountant.
4. Every music lesson formally ends with *sa pa sa*.
5. This is an inversion of the saying, *kuzhukkum acai micaikkum acai*, 'You can't eat the gruel without wetting your moustache.'

Payasam

Samanadu was standing in front of the platform around the pipal tree. He looked at the stone image of Pillaiyar on the platform. As is the custom, he knocked lightly on his temples. Then he bowed, up and down, a few times, his arms crossed, touching his ears, as the ritual demands.

'Why don't you bend your knees and do a proper bow? Who has the strength that you do? Are you sickly like Subbarayan, every day a crisis? You don't suffer from arthritis or blood pressure or vertigo, like he does.' It was as if he heard someone saying that, but no one was speaking. It was his own voice he was hearing. The same voice went on: 'I'm seventy-seven. Subbarayan is only fifty-six. But people would think it was the opposite. So what if he is worth fifteen to twenty lakh? Whose chest is as tough as the bottom of a coconut frond? Whose calves and arms are firm as rock? He's invited the whole world to his daughter's wedding. What are you going to do after finding the right match and marrying off your last child with the drums, the tying of the tali, and a big send-off with food for the journey? You'll be eating hot gruel for dinner along with your pills! And bathing in hot water in the morning. Can you walk, just once, to the Kaveri, swinging your arms, and immerse yourself for even a moment, like me?'

Samanadu looked around. The leaves of the pipal tree were rustling, as if saying something. Men, women, and children were passing by on their way to the river or coming back. Most of them were new faces. On the way there, the women had fine silk saris and empty pots. On the way back, there was *slup-slup* of wet saris and full pots. As they walked, drops of water formed beads of pepper on the sand. A child, five or six years old, slim as a green stalk, had bathed and was walking naked. Four or five men had changed, after bathing, into fine well-laundered, ironed veshtis with hems of Salem silk.

'A wedding today!' said one of the well-laundered veshtis, loudly.

'Yes indeed.' With a question in his eyes, Samanadu looked at the face. In his mind, he was asking, 'Why are you shouting? Do you think I'm deaf?'

'Don't you recognize me?' asked the fine-hemmed veshti. 'I'm Sita's brother-in-law, from Madurai.'

'Oh—now I recognize you. For a moment, I couldn't place you. I guess you haven't yet had your breakfast. Go ahead. You must have travelled all night in the train.' Samanadu was being polite.

'He's Subbarayan's uncle. He's the senior-most elder in the family. He's the one who presides over all the ceremonies.' The Madurai veshti introduced him to another well-laundered veshti. Samanadu went ahead.

Madurai was completing the introduction, but Samanadu sent them off, saying, 'You carry on, I'll be there after my bath.'

His mind spoke. 'Sita's brother-in-law, is it? Subbaraya, how did you manage to produce seven daughters? And marry them off after inviting trainloads of in-laws? God knows how many more brothers-in-law I have to meet before I step into the Kaveri!'

Leaving the pipal tree behind, Samanadu strode in the direction of the river. He lifted up the edge of his veshti and tucked it in at the waist, baring his calves, so that he could move quickly. He looked at himself—the thin towel on his right shoulder, a broad, open chest, gaunt stomach, eyes still without cataracts, good hearing.

Even before his feet touched the sand on the riverbank, he heard the sound of the wedding drums. The nagaswaram had already begun to play. The auspicious moment for the wedding was fixed for 10:30. It was not yet 8:00. The musicians were warming up. They needed to pass the time. Just to pass time, Subbarayan had produced seven daughters and four sons.

The river was almost in full flow. There was a sandy patch before reaching the water. He crossed it, his feet squishing in the sand.

The sound of the drums diminished. Soon they would be searching for him. He was the family elder. Subbarayan or his brother would come, calling for him, as if he were the master of ceremonies . . . Let them call . . .

Samanadu looked to his left.

The new bridge across the river—is that Subbarayan walking on it? No . . . Many people are crossing. A lorry, fully loaded bullock carts, pedestrians—all of them look like Subbarayan, even the lorries and the bullocks. It was Subbarayan who had brought the bridge to the village. If he had not used his influence with the government, they would have built it forty miles farther down.

To the right and behind, in the Velala farmers' street, smoke was rising from the jaggery vats. Beyond that lay the sugar cane fields. The sugar cane flowers were in bloom, glowing like oysters in the early morning sunlight. If he looked closely, they, too, looked like Subbarayan. After all, it was Subbarayan who introduced sugar cane to the village. Now, in front of him, too, on the opposite riverbank, smoke rose in four places from the cauldrons. All of it was Subbarayan.

And the school—Subbarayan.

And the cooperative right next to the bridge—Subbarayan.

He heard a voice. His wife's, carried by the wind. From seven or eight years ago—speaking directly to him, not much to his liking. 'Why are you boiling over? He's your nephew, after all. For twenty years, after I took your hand and stepped into your house, all I had was leftover rice, a little sauce, and these coral beads. What else could you give me? Could you or your brother send Subbarayan even four rupees a month for school fees? You and your brother sent him to study in Malaikkottai; you had him put up by some relative. And he studied well, but you didn't even let him finish. He was so close to finishing, but in the final year, you and your brother dragged him back here to the village. Why did you do that? The boy came back feeling frustrated and angry. He ran around everywhere looking for work, roasted by the sun. In the end, Lakshmi, the goddess of fortune, started dancing in his house.'

True, we couldn't give Subbarayan a good education. He came home. Then he ran away. He sat in a shop in Malaikkottai, doing accounts. Then he had a fight. He took a loan from one of the customers and set up a grocery shop that sold at half price. What a lucky fellow! Was it his face or his character? The small shop went wholesale; he started trading in truckloads of paddy and pulses. In twenty years, he had made twenty lakhs. He bought up a quarter of the village lands.

Then they partitioned the property, and he gave Samanadu half. Samanadu was angry. His half was located at a little distance. Not only that. None of it was close to the riverbed. Samanadu disputed the division. That's when Valambal, his wife, intervened. 'As if *you'd* given it to *him*, and now you're claiming it back. It's not something that your grandfather or your father had earned. Subbarayan worked hard and earned it all by himself. He took pity on you and gave you half. You don't count the teeth of a gift-cow or inspect its tail. Just take what he's given you. People in the village will laugh if they hear of this. If I were one of the village elders . . .'

'Even now you're not on my side. The way you're dancing by his side, in sympathy! Are you my brother's wife or mine? I don't understand you.'

'*Tu*, enough. You're being a damned fool,' said Valambal, moving away.

He guffawed in his stupid pride. Then he tried to make up with her. 'Don't be mad. I was just testing you.'

'Don't talk to me.'

She didn't speak to him for three days because of that silly joke.

Until she died, there were no further disputes over the property. The partition was accepted. What else could he do?

But he didn't get his full share of life. Valambal left this world. The first two sons she bore are no more. The third child, a daughter, is also gone. The fourth one got married and lost her husband after three years; she returned home. As is the custom, her hair was shaven; they made her wear the widow's brown, rough sari. Her wedding had taken place together with that of Subbarayan's third daughter. Samanadu's fifth child, a son, is a painter in Delhi. The sixth one is running errands at the wedding of Subbarayan's seventh daughter. He's the one who sent Samanadu off to bathe in the river and told him to hurry back, because he was the family elder.

Samanadu entered the river and immersed himself.

He saw a bus crossing the bridge. On top of it were bundles of banana leaves, a bicycle, four or five heavy bags, and stalks of sugar cane—all of them, again, were Subbarayan. Samanadu ground his teeth. 'What if I grabbed him by the neck and strangled him so his eyes would pop out . . . And all those children should be tied up in a sack.'

'Right, you have to drown all of them in the Kaveri. Only then can you go to hell, never to return. Go, right now.'

Her again. Valambal. As if she were right here, washing clothes on the rocks. Dark skin, wavy hair; the coral beads. Ruby studs in her ears. No sari blouse. Neither fat nor thin. He used to watch her bathe from a distance. He watched her from the corner of his eye, as if she were a stranger. Once when she came out and was changing, carefully hiding her breasts, thighs, and waist, she noticed him looking at her, and he looked away, embarrassed, as if he'd done something wrong.

He can still see it. Oh why did she go ahead of him to the world above?

One day she shook him up, right here in the Kaveri. 'He's given us half of what he earned. The other half he divided between his younger brother and himself. So his son will get only a quarter of a quarter. Why are you always burning with jealousy?'

What a devil she was! Right up to her last breath—what a sense of fairness! What a feeling for right and wrong!

'You kept me human, my love . . . Now you're gone,' he groaned. Tears, too, came to his eyes. He turned around. The next laundry stone was far away. Nobody could have heard. And even if they had, it would have sounded like a prayer.

Reciting the prayer '*narmade sindhu kaveri*', he wrung out his towel, wiped his body dry, straightened out the cloth and tied it around his waist. He smeared sacred ash on his forehead and started back. Subbarayan, poor fellow, would be calling for his uncle.

Now he could hear the nagaswaram and the drum from close up. He stood for a moment, bowing to Pillaiyar and the snake stones under the pipal tree. Then he hurried back into the street.

The whole village was dressed up like a bride. Everyone was going from house to house with brand-new saris, jewels, fair faces, fair feet, and calves. Some people were playing cards on the pyol. The street was filled with newly laundered silk veshtis and the hubbub of children playing.

Samanadu said to himself, 'Weddings of people from Manalur are the real thing.' His family was not originally from this village. Three generations back, his forefathers came here from Manalur to work as priests. They settled in a tiny house at the corner of the Brahmins' street. Now they own two big houses next to one another in the middle of the street. They still carry the tag of Manalur. Everyone in the village could see, just by looking at Samanadu and the way he carried himself, how the Manalur lineage had prospered—how it had surpassed the locals.

His own house and Subbarayan's house were like brothers. The pandal stood at the entranceway to both the houses. New veshtis on the pyol, and inside, noisy children, suitcases, and women with their hair put up in buns, decorated with flowers.

He went in past all of them. He put on a fresh veshti. In the backyard, he washed his feet, came back in, and sat down for his chanting. In earlier days, the four walls of the puja room were hung with pictures of Krishna, Rama, Pillaiyar, and other gods.

Now Krishna, Rama, and Pillaiyar have shifted to a small shelf. Now the walls were full of Madhu's paintings.

Madhu—his third son—hadn't come for the wedding. How many weddings could he attend for all of Subbarayan's daughters and sons?

'Appa!'

His daughter was calling him, her head covered, wearing the widow's sari.

'They're about to exchange the garlands. You can do your chanting tomorrow.'

'OK, OK, I'm coming now.'

She looked at him up and down. Confused.

'You go on. I told you I'm coming, didn't I? The same old thing . . .' She didn't hear the last words.

The shaven head. Thirty-one years old. But only twenty, if you look at her cheeks and her eyes.

'Why aren't you going? I told you I'm coming.'

She went off, closing the door quietly. He felt a burning in his throat.

He looked around. Madhu's paintings. He studied them closely. He smiled. One painting was only of a leg up to the knee. An eye on top of it. On the eyelashes, a comb. Another painting looks like a young woman, but one leg was a pig's leg. She is tearing her stomach open. Inside there are four knives, a can of powdered milk, and a foetus curled in the womb. Another painting—a lotus flower with a sandal on it. A moustache in the middle of it.

What's all this? He stood there staring, his mind frozen. His feet were hurting. 'Even my feet . . .?'

The music again.

'Appa, they're calling you'—the widow's head peeped in. That youthful face.

'OK.'

Samanadu went outside.

'Uncle, where did you disappear?'

Subbarayan's voice, gasping. His back hunched.

The bride and groom are exchanging garlands. They say that if one looks at the whole scene, they'll receive the merit of seeing Parvati and Shiva, or Lakshmi and Narayana. Even the widows were watching from the corners. Wherever you look, there are teeth. A broken tooth, a stained tooth, a worn-away tooth, a widow's tooth, a child's toothless teeth. Even the cook had come out.

'*Kannuncaladi nindrar*:[1] Swinging on a beautiful swing.' Somebody was singing.

The nagaswaram player also played the song. Samanadu was gasping for breath. He moved away slowly. He was burning with sweat. He went towards the backyard for a breath of air. Not a soul was there inside the house. He passed through the doorways and reached the backyard. There, too, there was no one. Hot coals were burning in clusters in the open trench ovens. Huge pots were left on the ovens, boiling with water. Behind a gunny screen, a young boy, grimy with sweat and oil, his sacred thread also full of grime, was slicing cucumbers. No other living creature anywhere nearby. All those fellows in the kitchen had gone to see the swing ceremony and the exchange of garlands.

By the side of the trench, on a low platform, stood a heavy vat, waist-high, full of fragrant payasam. Raisins and fried cashew nuts were floating on top. How could they manage to take it from the fire and put it there? Only by inserting a long pole through the ring handles, and then they needed two men to lift it. Enough payasam for five or six hundred people.

I can topple it over all by myself.

Samanadu held his breath and tried to budge the top of it. Oh. Is that all? The next moment, the vat, which had been standing with its mouth open to the sky, was lying on its side. The payasam was flowing into the gutter.

The boy who was slicing the cucumbers came running.

'Grandpa, Grandpa!'

Samanadu felt as if his face and skin were prickly like sand.

The fellow is running with the cutting blade in his hand.

Samanadu's hands and legs were shaking. He stammered in confusion.

'You bloody bastards, where the hell did you go? You left a big rat swimming in the payasam. Did you make all that payasam just for the gutter? You idiots, couldn't you have covered it with a plate?'

A maid came running.

'What happened, sir?'

'Yes. If "sir" hadn't noticed, you would have got rat poison instead of payasam. Go, all of you, put on your garlands and play on the swing.'

Another four or five people came running. His daughter, too, in her widow's clothes.

The maid explained to her what happened. ‘How did you overturn that huge vat, Appa?’

Doubt spread through her youthful face and body.

A shout. ‘Get out of the way. If it wasn’t for me, we’d have eaten rat poison, not payasam.’

She glared at him. Can eyes grow thorns?

Samanadu couldn’t bear to see the thorny bush. He turned his face away and lunged inside the house. ‘Where is that damned cook?’

The nagaswaram player was still playing the swing song in Anandabhairavi raga.

As if Valambal were singing it.

Note

1. At Brahmin weddings, after the exchange of garlands, the bride and groom swing on a swing, and this song is sung to the god and goddess, whom the young couple embody.

Crown of Thorns

'Now, with your permission, we will take our leave.' As soon as Kannusamy stood up, the crowd of students that had packed the hall also stood up.

'May I go, too?'

'May I go, too?'

'May I go, sir?'

In the midst of it, one boy touched the teacher's feet and brought his fingers to his eyes.[1] Anukulasamy instinctively drew back.

'What's all this, *tambi*?'

'Let him do it, sir. Who will they ever find like you? Please bless them; it will come true,' said Kannusamy.

After that boy, all the others, one by one, touched Anukulasamy's feet.

Anukulasamy stood there, feeling small.

'All this . . .' Anukulasamy was about to say something, but Kannusamy interrupted him. 'Anukulasamy, you're a true Christian. I'm not saying this to flatter you. To be a teacher for thirty-six years without once touching the cane, without raising your voice . . . what's wrong with falling at your feet in reverence?'

'Don't say such things.'

'It's not me saying it, the whole village says it. I get to know everything from just sitting in the bazaar. There's no one who doesn't beat his own son once in a while. Or scold him. But not you, no way. Who else could be like that? Children and gods reside where they are celebrated.[2] You treated these children and so many others like human beings.'

While Kannusamy was saying all this, the boys went on bending down to touch his feet. Anukulasamy wasn't able to get a word out. If he were to open his mouth, his voice would break, and his tongue would falter.

'May I go now?'

'Please do.' With some effort he opened his mouth and immediately closed it.

'With your permission, we, too, will go,' said the nagaswaram player, with folded hands, from the courtyard. Anukulasamy could only manage to nod his head.

It took two full minutes for the whole crowd to exit via the outside door.

Two or three boys, whispering to one another, said to him, 'Sir, please let us leave these two lamps here; we'll collect them tomorrow morning.' Then they left.

After he saw them off at the door and came back, the hall seemed desolate. Only once before had he felt such emptiness and this piercing longing. It was ten years ago, when he had taken Louisa to his son-in-law's house and returned home. The same emptiness; the same longing.

The two petromax lights filled the emptiness with their hissing.

They had gone away and left him alone. Tomorrow is Wednesday. But for him, Saturday, Sunday, tomorrow, the next day, the one after that—from now on, there will only be Saturdays and Sundays. He can't attend school any more. He had turned sixty and retired from service.

He sat down on the swing. Nearby, there were seven or eight framed testimonials; a silver plate and a pen, priced at barely four rupees in the shop. But here that pen was priceless. If you were to say it was worth four lakh or four crore rupees it would make no difference.

There were coils of four or five rose garlands with coloured straps and silver cords wound around them.

Makimai was there, holding the two chains of the swing. She didn't speak. She stood there, looking at him. She looked as if all the celebration and emotion were for her. For a minute, she drank him in. Suddenly she went to the entrance and bolted the door. Then she placed each of the garlands around his neck, held him by the shoulders, and gazed at him intently.

'You also never hit me and never spoke a harsh word,' she said, putting her head on his chest.

'We are only in this world for a short while, like termites before the rains. Should we waste that time hitting out and getting angry? Can you fix someone by hitting him?'

'You don't have to go mad like a demon. A man can get angry once in a while.'

'Of course, one can.'

'But you have to show it.'

'For that you have your milkmaid and house maid. Why should I add to it?'

'At your school, is it possible never to hit or speak a harsh word?'

'It was possible for me.'

Makimai looked at him in rapture, tucked at his moustache, and asked, moving away, 'Would you like some coffee?'

When she hurried inside, it was as if another body was carrying off his life force. He looked at the wall. That face with its crown of thorns was flooding him with compassion. Farther down, after four or five other pictures, there was another one where the same figure was hugging a lamb.

What Kannusamy had said was exactly true. In thirty-six years as a teacher, he had never once hit a boy or been harsh.

That was his nature.

Louisa was born. She went to school at the age of six. Once she was beaten by her teacher for some mischief. He hit her with a ruler that landed on a hot-season boil under her shirt. She screamed in pain.

When he saw this, Anukulasamy's nature became a vow. *He who gave his life for everyone's sins gave it for all generations.* That vow remained unblemished for thirty-six years. Was any other teacher brought all the way home from school in a procession on the day he retired?

The forty students in his class must have thought that the previous day's formal send-off was not enough. As a result, they had another gathering today. One garland after another. One testimonial after another. They were interspersed with the hum of the drone and the sound of the tavil on the veranda.

'Why all this, *tambi*?'

'For who else would we do this, sir? Please come.' A grown-up student, taking the lead, invited him. That Arumugam was twenty-three years old. He had not yet completed his schooling. He'd been at the school for many years. But he was worldly wise. Anukulasamy, without protesting, gave in to his request. If he hadn't, Arumugam would have started talking about other teachers. In fact, he'd already begun.

'Don't you know, sir? You didn't ask us to raise money because you are retiring. You didn't pawn a gilt jewel. You didn't raise the ire of the village by getting loans against a letter.'

Anukulasamy had to distract him. 'Let that be. Please bring me some water.'

Although he had to shut him up, what he said was true. He didn't incur the ire of the village. What's the difference if you slap someone or if you purposefully default on a loan?

He never tormented anyone like that.

Naranappayyar was a teacher like him. He didn't have a big family. One son and one daughter. But he was mired in debt. He reached the point where he didn't get an iota of respect, from the textile merchant down to the vendor of coriander leaves. Even then, Naranappayyar didn't keep quiet. A relative of his working in the office of the Director of Education in Madras wrote him a letter that said, 'You've been selected as one of the examiners this year. You'll receive an official letter within a week or two.' With this letter, he managed to get loans of fifty and seventy-five rupees from some twenty people. He was supposed to earn a measly two hundred rupees from that work. In the end, what the letter said didn't happen. Then he was done for.

Nayudu, the jeweller, cornered Naranappayyar and took away his bicycle. He was mad that he'd been cheated. Taking the bicycle wasn't such a big deal. Who would ride it anyway? But he was a teacher! Mister Naranappayyar, who had brought shame upon all teachers.

Could just anyone cheat the bank agent Ayyangar? He's so clever that he makes butter from churned buttermilk. Saminathan tried to trick that Ayyangar. Because Saminathan was a teacher, Ayyangar believed him and loaned him three hundred rupees against a chain of nine sovereigns. Saminathan should have stopped at that. If he brought another chain fifteen days later, would anyone give away money without testing it on the touchstone? As Ayyangar was testing the chain on the touchstone, he said with a smile, 'So, sir! If a boy asks a question in school, you can shut him up and tell him to sit down, hiding your ignorance. But will that work in the marketplace? Maybe I'm the one who doesn't know. Please wait a moment, I'll fetch the goldsmith.' Ayyangar went out. Saminathan's stomach churned. Couldn't he have sent a boy to fetch the goldsmith? While he was searching for some excuse, the goldsmith arrived.

Also the head constable. When they opened the safe vault in the presence of those witnesses, the chain pledged earlier said, 'I am brass.' Even at that moment, Ayyangar showed respect to the community of teachers. Without anyone's knowledge, Ayyangar got Saminathan to make over to him his fifty kuzhis of garden land, and he let Saminathan go. Luckily, the head constable had not come in his uniform. There was no crowd. Saminathan narrowly escaped becoming a laughing stock.

Now Anukulasamy remembered another four or five teachers. There was Ramalingam, who announced to his students, 'Listen. I've retired. From now on, no full meals. In my time, we collected funds for our teacher . . .' He managed to cajole one boy to make the rounds for him.

Makimai came with coffee.

'What are you thinking about? Have your coffee while it's hot.' She started reading the testimonials one by one. From time to time, she looked up with pride at Anukulasamy.

'Don't take them at face value. Since I won't be coming to work any more, they're trying to flatter me. It's all sugar and peppermint.'

'I know. But they're all telling the truth,' said Makimai. 'It's true that you never raised a hand or raised your voice.'

'Tsa—some truth!'

'But it's true to say that you have a talent. It's not so easy to earn a good name without raising a cane or speaking harshly.'

Anukulasamy thought it over. He felt there was some truth in it. It seemed to him that he had some right to feel proud.

'It's not that hard. One can be kind even to the milkmaid or the sweeper. Anyone born as a human being, anyone who has any sense, can't believe in violence.'

'Not everyone!'

'Well, I've been like that.'

There was a knock at the door. 'Sir.'

'Who is it?'

'It's me, sir.'

Makimai opened the door.

'Is sir at home?'

'Yes. Who is it? Is it Arumugam? Come in.'

Arumugam did not come alone. There was another boy with him. A boy in the same class. Also a lady. Must be around forty. Her forehead, ears, nose and arms were bare. Anukulasamy stood up.

'What news, Cinnaiya?'

'She's Cinnaiyan's mother, sir,' said Arumugam. 'Please come.'

If Arumugam brought someone, it must be for a recommendation. A twenty-three-year-old student, who had the clout of a village elder. It's hard to say why he came. It wasn't even examination time.

'What is it, Arumugam?'

'Cinnaiyan wanted to see you, sir.'

'What is it, Cinnaiya?'

Cinnaiyan didn't answer. He stood with his head bowed. Half a minute went by, and he didn't raise his head. He was crying.

The woman said, 'Tell him!'

Anukulasamy looked at him keenly.

The boy's face twisted, and his lips quivered.

'Go on, tell him,' said Arumugam.

'For a year he's been in agony,' said the mother.

'A year in agony?'

'Yes, sir,' said Arumugam. 'Now you can tell us that we can talk to him.'

'Tell me clearly. I don't understand anything.'

'Sir has forgotten,' said Arumugam, looking at the mother and at Makimai.

'What is it that I've forgotten?' Anukulasamy thought hard. Nothing came to mind.

Arumugam said, 'Sir, last year he stole Kayarokanam's English textbook, stuck another name on it, and sold it at the shop for half price. I was the one who found out and brought him to you.'

The boy was sobbing. 'Calm down,' said the mother.

'And then?'

'You looked at him for a while and then you said, "No boy in our class ever did anything like this. From now on, no one should speak with this fellow."'

The boy kept on crying.

'From that day on, we all avoided him, sir. Nobody spoke to him. We had a party today, right? We collected a rupee or two from each of the boys. Cinnaiyan also offered a rupee. We didn't take it. We also told him not to come to the party. He went away without saying a word. Today when I went home, he was waiting on the pyol with his mother.

His mother told me, and I brought them here.' Arumugam spoke haltingly, swallowing his words.

Suddenly he remembered. But—did I impose such a severe punishment? He had spoken without thinking much. But did they have to follow it so strictly?

He said, 'Cinnaiya, stop crying!'

'Please, sir, say that we can speak to him again.'

'For a whole year, he's been lifeless. He used to be happy and would laugh. Now he doesn't speak properly to anyone. He'll say just one word and go away. How can we know what is going on in his mind? He doesn't talk like he used to with his sisters. Only this evening he told me everything. The other children at home had gone off to play. He insisted that we should see his teacher. So I'm here. Please have a heart.' Cinnaiyan's mother spoke.

Anukulasamy felt as if he had been caught red-handed. His insides were squirming with pain.

'The other boys wouldn't take him with them. Please accept this with your own hand. When everyone is celebrating, he can't stay away . . . Cinnaiya, give it to him,' his mother said.

The boy's crying got worse. He extended his palm with the rupee soaked in sweat.

'Please accept it, sir,' Arumugam pleaded.

Anukulasamy took it without a word.

'He's a very good boy, sir. That day, his mind let him down. From then on, there has been no complaint against him.'

'You tell him, with your generous heart. If his friends won't speak to him, what will he do? They're only children, after all,' said his mother.

Anukulasamy said, 'I had no idea that these kids would do that to him.'

'They were only doing what you told them to,' said Makimai.

'That's true,' he said, smiling weakly. That smile camouflaged a sob. The crown of thorns in the picture above him pressed down, once, on his head.

Notes

1. A traditional gesture of reverence.
2. A proverbial statement.

The Mendicant

Vakkil Anna surveyed the rows of guests seated at the feast.

As for my humble self, I am not his real brother. Not even a brother once removed. The whole world, admiring his profound knowledge, happily and wholeheartedly called him 'Anna'.[1] In the same way, I'm his younger brother. The same street, the house across from his—that's the only kinship we shared. For that very reason, I'm a brother much closer to him than anyone else. The brother who comes running whenever called. I was his favourite brother, the first person to know what he thought about Eisenhower running for election or a young musician's concert.

Anna looked carefully at one row after another. With an eagle eye, he was scrutinizing the arrangements for the feast made by Junior Pappa Pantulu, me from the opposite house, the two clerks, and the young boys from the neighbouring houses who were waiting to serve like Lord Siva's attendants. Everyone wanted Anna to be satisfied. Junior Pappa, like a dog that had strayed into an unfamiliar street, was accompanying him, cowed and trembling. Anna's majestic look was measuring up everyone's status with approval.

Anna was a lawyer at court but a judge in life. He had extricated murderers and robbers, hovering between life and death, from the jaws of the law and given them refuge. Whether it was a midnight robbery or a heinous crime, when Anna argued a case, spraying words like a waterfall, the judge's individuality and impartiality were washed away. Such a man, a judge in life, will not let even a minor fault or a tiny slip pass. He won't rest until he has uprooted and pulverized that deed with the deviousness of Chanakya.[2]

The day before yesterday, the wedding of Anna's son took place. The next evening, all the guests had returned. The morning after that, the bride was ceremonially brought to the groom's home. The bride had arrived. Everything went off in a grand way. The only son!

The banana leaves had been spread for the feast. In the vast hall that could hold one hundred and fifty leaves, they had crammed another fifty. The backyard, the kitchen, the passages at the back of the house and in the front—wherever you looked, there were banana leaves. The rows in the hall were for hand-picked guests. In Anna's estimation, these two hundred belonged to the highest class. Junior Pantulu and I had carefully selected these guests.

Anna looked around imperiously. He's a judge in life. Even the slightest slip is still a slip. The smallest false note is still a false note. Anna is not merely a lawyer. He is a great connoisseur of music. Even more than a connoisseur, you could say he is a seasoned critic. He knows and delights in the depths of Carnatic music. He knows the texts of Venkatamakhi and Sarngadeva inside out. He has an intimate knowledge of the ancient Tamil scales. Wherever a music conference was taking place, in whatever corner of Madras Presidency, he'd be there. Someone drew a cartoon showing Anna's shiny head as he was demonstrating, only in words, the intricacies of a raga. That cartoon, enlarged, is hanging in his office.

Not just anybody's singing would please him. He thought that no one among contemporary musicians came anywhere near the threshold of his musical ideal. There was a woman singer in his village of Pukkalkulam. Her singing satisfied him. She was the granddaughter of the daughter of a disciple who was the grandson of a great composer who lived a century and a half ago. Now married with three children, she's a housewife living in Hyderabad. She's going to give a concert to welcome Anna's son's bride into her new home. She's come from Hyderabad just for this . . .

Somehow, we have strayed from the subject of the false note. Not only a false note in music, even a false note in words must not reach Anna's ears. Before the wedding, the workmen were putting up the pandal for the welcoming ceremony. It was 8.00 in the morning; the clerks had not yet arrived. A beggar happened to come by. Even the shadow of a beggar shouldn't have come anywhere near

Anna's house. Some newcomer. He was strumming an improvised drone, singing in a voice perfectly blended with the drone note.

'Come, Kamakoti, who lives in the great city of Kanchi, give me your boon with vankshai.'

'Hey, sing that again.'

'Come, Kamakoti, with vankshai . . .'

'What's that?'

'With vankshai.'

'What's that again?'

'With vankshai . . .'

'Is it vanchai or vankshai?'

'It's vankshai, sir.'

'Not vanchai?'

'No, sir.'

'Why is that?'

'My revered teacher taught me like that.'

'And who is your revered teacher?'

'Muruga Pandaram.'

'Where is he now?'

'He has attained samadhi.'[3]

'Good for him. From now on, you say vanchai.'

'But he always said vańkshai.'

'Then you won't get any rice.'

'No need, sir.'

'Try asking me for rice, and we'll see if you get it.'

'You try asking me to ask for rice. Just see if I ask.'

'You street dog, go away. Don't talk back.'

'Now who's barking?'

'Get the hell out of here.'

'Hey you, go away. You came here to beg and now you're spoiling for a fight,' the workman who was putting up the pandal butted in. 'Go away. . . . Sir, why get into an argument with this guy? He may say something very foolish. Why do we need this?'

'He says that's how his teacher taught him, and he won't change it.'

'That's exactly right! I won't change it. A word is made by man. If four hundred people call a crow a parrot, then it's a parrot, believe me.'

'Go away. . . . Get out of here. If you don't . . .'

That was the moment I arrived. 'Leave him alone, he's an idiot.'

'Who, him? You're the idiot. He argues point by point. And you call him an idiot. He's a stubborn ass.'

'Let him get lost, Anna.'

Anna is a judge in life and in words. No doubt about it.

Anna moved down the rows, inspecting them. Suddenly, his face darkened. He knitted his brows, and his nostrils flared.

'Hey, Panjami!'

'Anna . . .'

'Come quickly.'

I ran to him. 'Who's that? Where?'

'Over there.'

A mendicant was sitting in the row in the passage leading up to the hall, near the doorway. He was past middle age, had stepped into old age. He was all skin and bones. With a shock of grey hair, too white for his age, and an unkempt beard that entirely hid his cheeks. Chronic hunger made him look even older. A crumpled veshti with too many patches, yellowed from constant washing. Next to him was a bundle of the same colour. Despite all the precautions, he was sitting there like Rahu coming to feast on the ambrosia.[4] Lord Vishnu, who had taken on the ravishing guise of Mohini to carry the pot of ambrosia, had lost his senses for a moment. But would Anna be deceived?

'How the hell did he get in?' Anna shouted.

What answer could I give except silence?

'What brilliant management! Get this donkey out of here!'

'But he's already seated, Anna,' I mumbled.

'Is that so? Excuse *me*!' Anna dashed over and stood before the banana leaf. All two hundred faces stared at him.

'You there, get up!'

Without a word, the mendicant looked up at him. The mouthful of curry and rice was still in his mouth, and his fingers, smeared with food, were resting on the leaf. He looked at Anna in silence.

'I said get up.' Again, that famished look.

'Didn't you hear me?'

'I'm hungry. I just had one bite.'

That was the last straw.

Swiftly, Anna grabbed his hair in an iron grip.

'I'm telling you to get up. You're talking back, and you're still sitting there.'

The grip was so strong that the mendicant's hand automatically picked up his bundle, and his feet rose of their own accord. Anna dragged him with his left hand, pulling him hard by the hair across the passageway, then across the pyol and the pavement outside and down the steps, then tossed him past the pandal. The mendicant fell on his face in an awkward heap, his hair coming loose.

'*Aiyee*, *appa*, *amma*, you devil!' He picked himself up, groaning. He turned and looked at Anna. His face was red hot. Burning hunger blazed in his eyes. That fire flamed up from his face. His hand, full of food, had come so close, a little bite had even made its way into his mouth, stoking the hunger, and then this. Choked by helplessness and rage, his breath coming in small spurts, his stomach drawn in, he let out a fierce cry.

'You wretched lawyer, this will finish you off. Like a soldier of the god of death, you pulled me up and dragged me away when I had just sat down and barely had a bite!'

'Will you go now, or shall I break your bones?'

His eyes shooting flames, he shouted in a long, drawn-out voice, like the minister Chanakya taking a vow.

'I'm going, I'm going now. You can see I'm going. But I'll be back. Next month on the same date, I'll come to have a meal in your house. A meal you'll serve with tears. Just wait!'

Quickly, he walked off.

I felt pierced in my heart. What a thing he had said!

A fierce rage possessed Anna. 'Hey, go and drag that guy back. We can't just let him go like that.'

'Anna, please go inside. You can't throw stones in a muddy puddle.' I hugged him tight and pushed him back inside. He couldn't escape my grip, so he slowly went in.

What ominous words! Obscene words! Too cruel to be heard on an auspicious occasion. Unpalatable. Everything went black, as if a drop of poison had fallen from above into milk as it reached my lips. I felt darkness inside. How could he have spoken those words? That cursed man. He cut the string of sweet music with his sinister sounds. My heart was beating hard.

'Why that sheepish look? Idiot!' Anna shouted at me.

In the evening, the concert was held as scheduled. Parvatam, from Pukkalkulam village, sang. A mellifluous voice. Deep knowledge. But you could tell from her voice that she was the mother of three; and that turned the composition into something third-rate. Anna sat in the front, keeping time with his hands, counting the beat with his fingers, and vigorously nodding his head in approval. Within two hours, he had let out two thousand 'Ahas!' It looked as if his head would fly off. Anna had a terrific imagination.

The bride and groom were listening, sitting on a sofa. In the middle of it, the groom went to the backyard. Ten minutes later, Anna's wife rushed over and called me.

'Panju, call Anna.'

Anna and I went into the house. In the kitchen, the groom was lying unconscious. Apparently, he had thrown up in the backyard. After that, it seems he mumbled that his head was spinning. When he came into the kitchen, he collapsed and lost consciousness. Women were standing around him. Anna's elder sister was fanning him.

Anna called him, 'My child! My child!' I called his name, Visvanathan.

He was totally unconscious. There was no response. 'Panju, what can I do?' said Anna, looking up at me from where he was sitting. I had never seen such fear in his face.

'It's nothing, Anna! I'll fetch the doctor. Don't worry.' I ran outside.

The doctor came. For half an hour he tapped on him, here and there. He gave an injection. Wrote out a prescription. The boy didn't wake up. The doctor himself brought in a senior doctor. They conferred in their medical mumbo jumbo.

What can one say? There was no sign of him waking up. Nothing but meaningless blabber. For seven or eight days, he didn't open his eyes. The local doctors and witch-doctors all visited him. Two doctors from Trichy and five or six from Madras! Finally, a specialist arrived by plane from Calcutta. He felt his pulse. 'We can say something definite only after forty-eight hours. If he wakes up, give him this medicine.' He wrote the prescription, took his thousand rupees, and left. When a specialist like him says something, how can it go wrong? On the third day, it was all over.

To me, it all looked like magic. So fast! Anna's only son. His dream. He was his whole world. Now in ruins. Anna sobbed. Suddenly, he would remember and cry aloud. When he wasn't crying, he'd sit staring into empty space. Suddenly, he would smile. It looked to me like a demon's grin. I was badly shaken.

'Panjami, you want to know why I'm smiling? Tomorrow is the fifth.[5] That's why.'

I didn't answer. I let him do what he wanted—smile, weep, wail in grief. Who can say what is happening in an unhinged, unsteady mind? Grief is the twin of deep love.

'Tomorrow is the fifth. Tomorrow, it will be twelve days since life left me. On the last fifth, we performed the welcoming of the bride. How did that wretched mendicant nail the date so precisely?'

There was no need to remind me. He had constantly been in my thoughts.

The next day, the twelfth day, the funeral rites were to begin in the morning. It was about 8.00. He came and stood at the door. He stood there like a corpse come alive. White beard, moustache, all skin and bones, yellow, frayed veshti, a bag in his hand—just as he had come to the wedding that day.

I was enraged, my heart seething. My hands were itching to wring his neck. But there was nothing

I could do. That burning rage turned into smoke and left me. My mind shuddered and went dead.

The moment Anna saw him, he started sobbing uncontrollably.

'Sir, don't feel bad. I didn't come to poke at the wound. I came because the word cannot be undone,' said the mendicant.

For a while, Anna turned his face away. With a great effort, gritting his teeth, biting his lips, wiping his eyes, he held in his grief. The mendicant just stood there, his head bowed. Five minutes passed.

'You—your word has come true,' Anna said.

'My word? What are you saying? What has to happen will happen.'

'It was you who gave the curse.'

'My hunger uttered the curse. But I don't think that was the only reason for what happened. I might have said something that was there, without our knowing it . . . Sound is everywhere. Are we able to hear it? We have to clap our hands or do something to hear it. It's like that . . .'

'Can you read the future?'

'No, I can't. I said what came to my lips.'

'Mm. You seem to be a man of knowledge. Why are you wandering around begging for food?'

'If a person has knowledge, does it mean he has to practise law? Even if I had some knowledge, wouldn't I still have to beg for food?'

'I don't understand.'

'How can you understand? You didn't have the courage to see me sitting and eating in the midst of all those big men. You weren't strong enough. Your sense of self is so fragile. It doesn't rest on a foundation of love. Cement looks weak. If you mix in water and let it harden, you'll need a sledgehammer to break it. Your heart of stone is actually a weak one. If you had mixed even a drop of love into that big ego, it would have stood firm. It would have had the fragrance of jasmine. There's no real strength in your heart. If you had it, would you have defended in court that Pandi who had committed a double murder in broad daylight? The whole world knows that he had murdered. You argued vehemently and saved him, but justice was not done. As I said, your pride has no strength. If it had been strong, you would have seated at the wedding those people who have cars, a thousand acres of land, and diamond studs along with this mendicant, along with poverty itself—and joy would have filled your ears, your eyes, and your heart. Your ego couldn't see beyond the cars and the diamonds.'

Anna sobbed, staring into space. After a while he said to the mendicant, 'Oh Lord of Death, why don't you sit down? Aren't your legs hurting?'

The Lord of Death, hunger embodied—stomach limp, eyes sunken, ribs sticking out—uttered the name of God and sat down.

Notes

1. Literally, 'elder brother'.
2. Chanakya was the legendary minister of Chandragupta Maurya, known for his Machiavellian devices.
3. A euphemism for the death of a teacher or a sage.
4. After the gods and the demons had churned the ocean of milk and the ambrosia had emerged, Rahu, the demon of eclipses, appeared and tried to snatch it from the hands of Mohini—that is, Vishnu in his feminine guise. Vishnu, at first bewildered, cut off Rahu's head.
5. The fifth day of the lunar month.

Ecstasy

The passenger train from Tirucciirappalli to Mayavaram. Its life starts at 10.30 in the morning and comes to an end at 3.00 in the afternoon. After seeing off trains to Madurai, Manamaturai, and Erode, Trichy Junction looked deserted, its empty platforms glowing in the sun, like a coconut grove ravaged by a cyclone. All you could see were banana peels, orange peels, empty food packets, and a few lousy lazybones. The train departs in half an hour. Still no sign of the engine or the guard. In coach after coach, someone unkempt and unwashed was sleeping. A family that had arrived on the Bangalore Express had left its luggage in the second-class compartment, with someone to look after it, and gone off somewhere. If it were an express train, what a crowd and what a welcome! And what a hullabaloo when it left. This passenger train was lifeless, with no one to care. The most forlorn of shuttles. It seems that in the caste of trains, too, there are rich and there are poor.

I was alone in the last coach but one. My son was next to me, fast asleep. Near his head was an orange that had slipped from his hand. When I looked at it, I smiled. I was bringing him home from Bangalore. When his uncle's wife came to visit us, she took him back with her. Then I went to Bangalore on business, so now I was bringing him home. His uncle, my brother-in-law, came to Bangalore City Station to see us off. Five minutes before departure, my boy saw a fruit seller and said softly, 'An orange, Appa, an orange.' His uncle looked the other way as if he hadn't heard. I know my brother-in-law. I glared at my son. He became silent. The moment the train left, he started up. A six-year-old child: how long can he keep quiet?

'Appa, Appa.'

'What, my son?'

'Picci Uncle earns 900 rupees a month. Like, he's rich. So rich.' He's stretched out his arms and lifted his chin, as if to complain.

'So what?'

'Just a minute ago, you know, I asked for an orange, didn't I? He just looked away.'

'Maybe he didn't hear you. If he had, he'd have gotten it.'

'But I said it out loud.'

'Then why didn't he get it?' I turned the question back on him. The boy struggled for words. 'Like, you know, I asked Picci Uncle to get me a tricycle. Then, you know, he kept saying he would, but he never did.'

'Why him? I'll get it.'

'How can you?'

'Why not?'

'You earn only a hundred rupees, right?'

'Who told you that?'

'Um . . . it was Picci Uncle.'

'He told you himself? That your father earns only a hundred rupees?'

'Uh-uh, not to me. He told Auntie. You sent a letter from Madras, on the day of Pillaiyar puja.

It was then. He said you keep going to Madras for nothing. You can't even afford a simple waistband.'

My God.

'It's time. Go to sleep.'

'Will you buy me a car?'

'I will.'

'Not a real one. A little one that you wind up.'

'OK, OK, I'll get it.'

'Appa, the orange.'

'Go to sleep. I'll get you one when we reach Trichy.'

'No, now.'

'Where could I get one now? The train is moving.'

'Then tell me a story.'

'That's better. I'll tell you a good one. Once upon a time . . .'

Halfway through the story, the boy fell asleep.

'He's a good boy. He's *shrewd*. Studies people well.' The man sitting across from us suddenly offered a certificate.

'That's why his head is so big!' I looked at the boy. His head really was a little big. A striking face. Well-proportioned. His body was a bit chubby. His skin shiny like a young sprout. On his cheeks, you could barely see the baby hair glowing in the light of the lamp. The hair on his head was all thick curls spilling over on to his forehead. You could call him beautiful. He is going to see his mother tomorrow at midday. Until then? I felt I was looking at an orphan. If a child is not with his mother, where does he get his lustre? I caressed him two or three times. How could Picci Uncle have the heart to disappoint this guileless child? From the day he started earning, he'd earned a name as a miser, hadn't he? And now even from this child? I wasn't able to just brush it aside. Whenever I looked at the boy, a sadness rose up in me. A petty incident. But I couldn't bear it. Picci Uncle survived by constantly cheating others; who he was inside never matched what he did. That's how he lived his life. Even at home with his wife, he was never sincere. In all this, he was a 'success'. These thoughts were swirling in my mind like a horde of bees, all night long. I couldn't sleep.

When we got to Trichy, I bought an orange. 'Appa,' he said, 'I'll eat it when we reach home. Amma will peel it for me, and I'll eat it.'

'All right.'

There was still half an hour before the train's departure. I was parched. I got down, drank some water, and chewed some betel.

When I got back to the coach, a woman was getting on. She had a girl with her. They sat down on the seat opposite us.

'This train is going to Mayavaram, isn't it?'

'Yes, it is.'

'When does it leave?'

'In twenty-five minutes.'

'How far are you going?'

'Up to Kumbakonam.'

'Your child?'

'Yes.'

'He's fast asleep.'

'We're coming from Bangalore. He's tired.'

'Aren't you going to lie down?'

'No Auntie, I don't feel sleepy,' said the girl.

'Have a little sleep, my child. We have the whole night to travel. And tomorrow, and the day after tomorrow.'

'No Auntie, I'll sleep later.'

The woman was about forty. She was fat. Bright like a Rumani mango. On her ear she had a big Blue

Jager stud, cut in the old fashion. A diamond stud on her nose. On her neck, a necklace with seven or eight strands. Just like that, bangles on her arms. She was wearing a mango-coloured silk sari. On her forehead, she had a dot of turmeric and vermilion. There was nothing jarring to the eye. Next to her were a leather box and a new iron charcoal stove.

The girl must be eight or nine. Of light complexion. All skin and bones. Limbs like sticks. Sunken eyes. There was no light on her face. Lethargic, drowsy eyes. She wore a rubber bangle. She was wearing a newly made cheap skirt, still stiff, and a red cotton blouse with printed flowers. It was also new. Around her neck, a chain of glass beads. Beside her, another cheap skirt, squished and rolled up. A blouse was stuck inside it.

How were these two related? How to ask?

When the train was about to leave, a fruit seller came with the famous Malappazham bananas. I bought a bunch and gave one to the girl. She took it without a word.

'Eat it.'

When the woman said it, the girl peeled it and ate it.

'This girl is going to Calcutta.'

'To Calcutta?'

'Yes. Someone from this side has a big job there. She's going to his house. Someone they know from Mayavaram is going to visit him. I have to hand her over to him. She's a good girl, obedient and capable.'

Then I started asking my questions.

'What's your name?'

'Kamakshi. They call me Kunju.'

'Good, very good.'

'What's so good about it?' The woman laughed. 'You wonder how this little body can carry two names!'

I also laughed.

'That's also true. But I was thinking about something else. I have a younger sister named Kamakshi. She looks like this girl. We married her off to a man from a well-off family. But the son-in-law is a very helpful sort. He stood guarantee for someone, for 20,000 rupees. That guy suddenly kicked the bucket. My sister's family collapsed. Her husband had a really hard time. You can't describe the suffering. Only for the last four or five years has he found a job and been free from harassment. Her problems are now over. There's another younger sister. Her name is Kunju. We moved heaven and earth to find her a husband. In the end, there was my cousin, a very sick woman with no children. She was insistent that we marry the girl off to her husband, so my father gave in. But from the day she got married, she suffered worse than a dog. After ten long years, she gave birth to a boy. That was three years back. It's only since then that she could hold her head high in the house, like a human being.'

'Whatever you say, how can you marry a girl to a man who already has a wife?'

'What could we do? It's our lot. When I heard the girl's name, I was reminded. I was surprised that she has both my sisters' names.'

I couldn't make out how the girl took all this in. She was listening and looking on with the same sleepy face without any sign of movement.

'Child, do you have your father and mother?'

'Yes.'

'What does your father do?'

'Teaches first grade.'

'Sisters and brothers?'

'Yes. Four older sisters, two older brothers, one younger brother and a younger sister.'

'Are all your older sisters married?'

'Three of them are. The second one lost her husband four years back. She lives with us.'

'What does your older brother do?'

'The first one works in a restaurant. The second one is in seventh standard.'

'Aren't you going to school?'

'No. Only my brother goes to school. My father can't pay the fees for all of us.'

'So you're going to work?'

'Uh-uh. We can hardly eat once a day.'

'What kind of work can you do?'

'I scrub the dirty dishes. I make coffee or tea. I grind batter for idli and dosai. I know how to make kuzhambu and rasam. I can look after children. I make kolams. I can take care of the mud stove. I can wash veshtis and saris.'

'You can wash a sari? Can you even lift one?'

'Yes, easily.'

'Where did you learn all of this?'

'There's a judge named Ramanathaiyar. At his house.'

'So you have experience. How many years were you there?'

'I've been there for three years.'

'Three years! How old are you?'

'Last Avani I completed nine, and now I'm going on ten.'

'So you started working when you were seven. My God. How much do you get?'

'Nothing like a salary. They give me two meals a day. And for Deepavali, a skirt and blouse.'

'Who got you this blouse?'

'They did.'

'For all that work—making kolams, maintaining the stoves, washing saris, looking after the kids, grinding the dosai batter—all they could give you was a lousy piece of cloth worth six annas? This measly rag was the best they could find?'

'. . .'

'Couldn't you have asked them to get you something better?

'. . .'

'You say you've been eating in the judge's house. It doesn't look like it. More like you've been in a famine, your eyes sunken and dry, as if a dog had gouged them out.'

'Don't you know that rich people are different? Half the time, they eat like paupers—watery kuzhambu, roasted pappad, rasam without dal. At night, some lentils and rice and rasam. But still, there's a glow about their bodies. It's a special kind of body. It wouldn't work for people like us, who live one day at a time. If we had this kind of food for two days, our mouth would be full of sores, our eyes sunken, and we'd be totally exhausted.' The woman included me in her description. Out of courtesy, of course. Suddenly, as if she'd said something wrong, she asked, 'I'm rambling on. By the way, what do you do?'

'It's all right. I also live one day at a time. I'm a clerk at the taluk office.'

We were approaching Tanjavur station.

'I'll leave this towel on my seat. Keep an eye on my place. I'll have something to eat and get something for my boy.'

'Oh, you haven't eaten?' Then, to the girl: 'What did you have in the morning?'

'Leftover rice.'

'Where?'

'At the judge's place.'

'Didn't I tell you? That's how rich people are. This girl who's been working for them for three years, stuck in their house—couldn't they at least give her a good meal before she set out? They brought her to me at quarter past nine. Couldn't they have cooked her something before that? Very generous people. As if they were afraid that their ritual of offering leftover rice would be broken. Does anyone else in that household eat leftover rice?'

'It's only me.'

'Umhum. Are you hungry now?'

'No.'

'Eat something.'

'OK, Auntie.'

'Please get a packet of sambar rice and curd rice.'

'I'll take the girl with me.'

'That's fine. Take this.'

'Why give me money? I'll pay.'

'You can't say no. I'm the one who is taking her.'

I felt uncomfortable. I took the money. I woke the boy. I dragged both of them, in a hurry, through the crowd to the canteen.'

'Who is this, Appa?'

'This girl is going to Mayavaram and then on to Calcutta. She's going to eat with you.'

While the two orphans were eating, a kind of pity rose up in me. Two orphans separated from their mothers. But what a difference! In two hours, one of them would be sitting happily in his mother's lap. The other one would be going farther and farther away.

'*Sss* . . . Appa, Appa!' the boy cried out. 'Hot chilli!'

'Here, drink some water.'

The girl rushed to the counter, took a handful of sugar and gave it to the boy.

After a bit she said, 'The curd rice is lumpy. Let me loosen it up. Then you can eat it.' She stopped eating, washed her hand, and broke up the lumps in the curd rice so he could eat it. The boy watched her, turned to me, and smiled.

'Why are you smiling?'

'She's squishing it for me.' That was all he could say.

She was the one who washed his hand and wiped his mouth.

'Here,' she said, 'drink some water.'

'No.'

'Otherwise, you won't digest the food. Drink up.'

Usually he'd make a fuss, but he took the water and drank it without a word. As if she'd been doing it for years, she took his hand and carefully led him back. He let himself be led.

'You say you're going to Calcutta. Do you know them well?'

'No, Uncle. They say he's got a big job. He earns three thousand rupees. They need someone to look after their kid. That's why they're taking me there.'

A child from somewhere is going to take care of a child from somewhere else. A mother is sending her child to some unknown place. The child, for her part, rolls up a skirt and sets off.

'She's a very clever girl,' I said to the woman.

'When there's no one there, you're bound to be clever. She takes to people easily. If she weren't going to Calcutta, I'd keep her myself. Didn't you notice? Until we asked her, she didn't open her mouth to say she was hungry. Only God should look after her.'

The boy again took the orange in his hand.

The woman asked, 'Shall I peel it for you?

'No need. When I get home, I'll ask Amma to peel it for me.'

'I'm a mother, too.'

The boy answered with a smile. Some minutes passed.

Suddenly he asked Kunju, 'How old are you?'

'I'm ten.'

'Ten? Then you must be in fifth class.' He was counting on his fingers.

'No.'

'If she's ten, does that mean she should be in fifth class?' I asked.

'Yes, Appa. I'm six. I'm in the first class. Six, seven, eight, nine, ten. She should be in fifth.'

'She's not in school.'

'You're not in school?'

'. . .'

'Studying at home?'

'Umhum.'

'She's going to Calcutta. That's why she's not in school.'

'Why is she going there?'

'She's going to work.'

'No way . . .' Then he asked her: 'Are you going to work?'

'Yes.'

The boy stared at her for a moment, unbelieving. He asked again.

'Can you ride a bicycle?'

The girl laughed out loud. It was the first time she laughed.

'How would I know how to ride? I can't.'

'So how will you get to work?'

'I'll walk.'

Again he looked at her, a little thoughtfully. He couldn't grasp how his father rode a bicycle to work, but she had to walk. How was it possible? Both children looked out at the open paddy fields, savouring the speed of the train.

'Who can this girl trust if she's going so far away? Who knows what kind of place she's going to?' I asked.

'The person she's going to is a brother-in-law once removed from the judge. They say he's getting three thousand, in some company. If it is someone from our place, they'll be dependable. Whatever you say, let's assume they'll give her good food and clothes. But however good they are to her, she'll still be a child from some other family, somebody who came there for work. And can she think of them as her mother and father? Look how she takes to people; I'm sure she'll manage anywhere. Still, will it be like staying with her parents? You tell me.'

My stomach churned. Emptiness and fear overwhelmed me, as if I were going to some unknown place where I had nobody.

'God will take care of her, too. Otherwise, how could her parents have sent her off, relying on human beings?' I said.

'Only God should take care of her. What else can we say? Again and again, we come round to Him. But who is bothered that a family has reached the point of sending her away? Who could fix *that*? If they paid the teacher the school fees for each of his kids, this girl wouldn't have to go to such a faraway place.'

'And who would look after the judge's kids?'

'That's also true.'

'Everywhere, it's the same story. Maybe the person who pays the teacher is also a pauper,' I said.

'It's all a mystery.'

Everyone in the compartment who saw the girl was moved. Everyone who got on the train at Tanjavur, Aiyampettai, or other stations was moved, even if they only heard a bit of the conversation. The man sitting at the far end of the seat where the woman was sitting—maybe a Saurashtrian—bit his lips and turned his head toward the window. You could see he was valiantly trying to contain the pain.

The train reached Kumbakonam.

I said goodbye to the woman. I said goodbye to the girl, too, pressing a rupee coin into her hand.

The woman protested. 'Why are you doing this?'

'I also have the right. You're also only taking her. She's the teacher's daughter, not yours. I have as much right as you do. What can I do? I feel like giving her something. I can't afford to give more.'

A huge sigh came from her heavy body. 'Take it,' she told the girl. 'Life will be good to you,' she said to me.

'Appa, let me give her this,' the boy said, showing me the orange.

'Just give it to her, don't ask.'

'No need, my child. He was waiting for his mother to peel it for him.'

'Appa, please ask her to take it,' he pleaded.

I said to the girl, 'Take it.'

She took it.

'Svami, what a fine child you have. Come, little boy. Give me a kiss before you go,' said the woman. The boy gave her a kiss and ran back to me.

A current ran through my body. I turned my face away so no one would see, got down from the carriage, took him in my arms and walked away. Couldn't he have walked by himself? Without knowing why, I felt I had to scoop him up and hold him tight. I walked on, hugging him to me, my heart surging. A vast ecstasy embraced me, alive in my arms.

Message

'What is it?'

Disgust and anger spilled over Pillai's face. 'Stop!' He raised his hand.

The sound of the nagaswaram stopped.

'What a nuisance! Even now, just before dawn! You were at it all night. I was resigned to it, but it's morning and you're starting up again. My own goddamned son. What's all this? This is the moment to sing Bilahari and Kedaram ragas to make the sky shower you with flowers. Why this lament? Are you crazy or what?'

The son sat there, stroking the nagaswaram, saying nothing.

'Have I taught you music so that you start this lament even before you rub your eyes in the morning? You might as well be chopping meat at the butcher shop on the street next to the river. What use is the nagaswaram to you? Why the drone? Why are you sulking like that? Does what I'm saying sound bitter? . . . Tell me. Answer me!'

'You said there's a concert today. That's why I was practising,' said the son at last, casually.

'Practising? . . . Hm!' That *hm* was biting. Pillai was so angry he wanted to slap him hard. The next moment, doubt arose. Maybe his son had lost his mind.

'You know who's performing?'

'. . .'

'I asked you something.'

'. . .'

'Answer me!'

'It's you.'

'Yes, it's me. Do you think I'd have you sit beside me and let you play that lament, that cinema song, that music that belongs nowhere, like a bandicoot scraping the spice box? Did you think you would blast out all that racket?'

'The audience is all white men.'

'So?'

'Isn't it better that we play something they can understand?'

'What are you trying to say? That they won't understand what I am playing? And just to save my good name, you're going to play something like these two pieces so that they won't think they came here for nothing.'

Tangavelu chose to remain silent, as if agreeing with what his father said. Even when his father's sarcasm whipped him again and again, he kept silent like a martyr, certain that truth was on his side.

'You know what Aiyar said? He wanted to have our music, only our music. That's what the guests wanted. How can we know now if they like it or not? You've already decided that they won't like it. They aren't coming to hear something they can understand. They just want to know what our music is like. Only when we play will we know whether they understand it or not. All you want is to play this racket and claim that it's our music. This is how you think you can save the honour of our music! Thanks for this huge concern . . .!'

The son smiled a knowing smile. The father smiled, too.

'Go rinse the instrument.'

Tangavelu put the nagaswaram in its cloth cover, tied the ends, hung it on a nail on the wall, and moved away. Pillai sat down on a bench close to the window, pulled out the screw-pine box, took out areca nut and started shaving slices.

That was the place where, for generations, instruments had been hung. The instrument that the son had been practising on was one which his father had played. It produced a tone that overpowered one's entire being. Whenever one recalls the Useni raga that he played in the Tiruccerai temple, it electrifies the whole body. Such power to move you. Full of life. Such profound engagement. An inflection that captures the subtlest layer of sound. It was on that same instrument that Tangavelu had been blowing out raucous, unruly notes.

For a year now, Pillai had been worried. At weddings, Tangavelu was belting out on the nagaswaram the cinema songs that you hear coming at you, wailing, from all directions. From the beginning, people had rejected Pillai because he couldn't entertain them. That didn't worry him. As long as he was receiving an annual grant from the temple managed by the mutt, he was confident his music would live on. He had enough to eat. Apart from food, there was a pair of veshtis for him, two upper cloths, four saris for his wife, and four veshtis for his son. The grant provided all of this. What more does a man need? That's what he didn't understand. Who needs big bracelets and a picture in the papers? For twenty-five years, ever since he grew up, time flowed past like this, without his paying heed to anyone. And now?

Tangavelu lacked nothing when it came to understanding music. His father, well aware of the fragility of the human body, hastened to engrave everything he knew, as quickly as possible, on his son's mind. But how did this damned idiot get it into his head that he had to please all those tasteless vagabonds and ignoramuses? Has music been condemned to ruin? When God himself is destroyed, how many days will His name live on?

The nagaswaram is hanging on that same nail in the same cloth cover. It is a heavy cover of raw silk from the time of his father. But the nagaswaram has become itself a cover for some other nameless thing.

'Are we making a mistake? Music that people don't understand—can you call it music? Can art that nobody understands still be art? Don't people invite us because what we play makes them happy? Is it fair that we wander off into another world, leaving them behind?'

It's a question he's been asking himself for years. For the last year, it's cropping up every day. Tangavelu, after elaborately playing the Malayamarutam ragam, suddenly piped out a clownish tune. Early in the morning . . . what discord! When Pillai heard it, he thought he was watching a monkey dancing, decked in a shirt and earrings.

Impelled by a sudden urge, Pillai quickly took off the cover and put the instrument to his lips. He couldn't catch that discordant note. A phrase not connected to any particular note made him gasp. A phrase like when you are lying on your back with a mouthful of water and you spit it out, and the drops fall on you in an arc. When he wondered what note that was, it refused to stay with the underlying drone and stood out. 'What kind of music is this? A note with no basis in the shruti?'[1]

'Damn!' he said. Though he felt disgusted, he tried again. Maybe it also calls for skill. That phrase was not within his grasp. The stubbornness of the phrase and his own stubbornness set off a battle. Gasping, Pillai smiled.

'Not like that, Appa . . . Like this,' he heard a voice.

The son stood at the door to the room, ready to teach his father the phrase, the way Lord Murugan taught his father Shiva the meaning of the mantra Om.

'Oh, yeah?'

'That phrase.'

'Play it once.'

The son played it.

'That awful note—which has no father—how do you manage to capture it? I can't do it.'

Pillai tried again. It didn't work.

'Like this?'

'That one is different.'

'That's our music.'

'And whose is this?'

'It's different.'

'From which country?'

'Who knows?'

Pillai tied his upper garment around his waist, prostrated along the whole length of his body, and stood up.

'Do you know who I'm bowing to? To that awful note. I won't ever look at it again.'

'What's this?' asked his wife, her eyes wide open in shock, when she brought him coffee.

'I'm bowing down.'

'To whom?'

'To the music of your dear son.'

'Amma, it's just a film song,' said Tangavelu.

'Why, can't you get it?' she asked her husband.

'Maybe if I offer milk to that song over a hundred lifetimes.' Pillai laughed.

They had an unspoken agreement, father and son. If, towards the end of a wedding procession, someone sends a note asking for a film song, Tangavelu would take charge. Pillai would retreat to some nearby porch.

At night, Tangavelu would practise these songs as and when they were released. That's why when Pillai heard it in the morning, he was startled.

Pillai looked at the nagaswaram.

White men! Music lovers! It seems they want to hear pure south Indian music.

Mani Aiyar, the lawyer, had said just the day before yesterday, 'They want to hear the kind of music that resonates in the heart like a big temple bell, that lingers on in your mind for a long time.'

'Why do they take all this trouble?' said Pillai. 'These days you have *imitation* curry leaves, *imitation* cooling roots, and *imitation* milk. Talk of purity in music! It's crazy.'

'The world isn't yet so far gone. Why are you so bothered? Listen to me. Just play. Four kirttanais should be enough. You don't even need the tavil accompaniment. Play for yourself, as if you were sitting alone. That's enough. No need to pay attention to what the listener is wearing or how he moves. Close your eyes and play two kirttanais. That will do.'

Pillai laughed. What a man.

'Do I have to wear a shirt or something?'

'As you like. Our guest seems to me dignified and unassuming. So what does it matter if you put on a shirt or don't?'

The concert is at six. Right from the moment he woke up, he started planning what to play. Tangavelu was practising his new song. It grated on Pillai's ear and ruined his concentration.

Setting aside his bitterness and his exhaustion, in search of quiet, he picked a raga and played it in his mind, amazed as he saw its form. His mind, his very self, were immersed in a flood of joy. In that state he fell asleep, leaning against the wall.

~

Pillai got off the single-bullock cart and entered the house of Aiyar, the lawyer. Tangavelu followed him with the drone players, carrying the instruments.

A big hall. The lawyer received Pillai at the entrance and took him by his hand to introduce him to everyone.

'This is Phillip Polska, the leader of this music group.'

Phillip Polska looked like a maharishi. About seventy years old. Not bald. With a shock of ruffled wild hair. Medium build. Big eyes. His pupils floating, with a faraway look. Blue eyes. They made you wonder if he was asleep or lost in thought. Pillai took one look at his eyes. Something tugged at his heart, as if it were caught in a knot. His heart leapt towards him.

'Do you remember that you said he was dignified and unassuming?' Pillai asked the lawyer.

'True.'

'You were right. Look at his eyes. Look at that handsome face.'

'I also thought so. Can I tell him what you said?'

'Better not. Let's keep it to ourselves. We don't have to flatter the foreigners. If he asks what I said, tell him I said I was very pleased to see him.'

After Polska, Aiyar introduced him to another twenty or twenty-five people.

The musicians mounted the platform and, as soon as the drone player began to play, Pillai adjusted his reed. Tangavelu sat down behind him.

Pillai played a majestic alapanam in Nattai raga. Then he started on the kirttanam.

A gentle smile played on Polska's face. The pupils of his eyes were glazed. It seemed that he had lost himself in the rising tide of delicious sound. As if the sound had carried his very self to other worlds and to experiences he had never known. Like someone who gives himself to the whims of a rushing stream.

The sound abruptly stopped. Polska's eyes were still immersed in the moment. It took a minute for him to focus them on Pillai.

The listeners were sitting cross-legged, with tie and trousers, watching Pillai.

'*Aiya*, I'm going to launch a little experiment,' said Pillai to the lawyer.

'What is it?'

'Just wait.'

The lawyer looked at him, a little lost. He couldn't make out anything from Pillai's face.

Pillai started to play: '*Dha sa ri ma . . . ma*.'

The lawyer recognized Sama raga. He looked intently at Pillai. Little by little, the raga began to unfold. Memories of coral jasmine, flowering at midnight with its quiet fragrance, drenched the lawyer's heart. His head swayed in harmony with that fragrance. The raga was swelling up.

He felt as if someone were moving his hands. He looked behind him. It was Polska, his body rocking along with the raga. He had stretched out his hands, as if receiving something. A light smile on his face. Like one possessed, he was staring into space, lost to time.

Suddenly, he stood up. Like a champak tree in a gentle breeze, he stood there, arms outstretched, moving slightly. The raga deepened further.

He took a step forward. Another step—as if he were holding the music in his hands. Slowly, he advanced towards the platform and, reaching it, knelt down. At the edge of the platform, he buried his face in his hands.

The lawyer and the other listeners were watching him. Who knows in what world Polska was wandering? In what universe was he?

Pillai was afraid that he was about to puncture that universe. Without even pausing for a moment his alapanam, he began the kirttanam.

'*Santamu lekha* . . .' The line caressed them as one caresses a child. As if seeking, pleading for the surpassing truth.

Polska broke out in goosebumps. His back quivered, a sudden jolt.

The kirttanam came to an end. The instrument became silent.

Polska, his face buried in his hands, took a small leap forward and grasped Pillai's hand with a pleading look.

Pillai didn't know what to do. He mustered a slight smile, as one might smile at a child.

'Mister Pillai, Mister Pillai,' Polska implored him, still holding his hand. His voice broke.

'Mister Pillai, please don't play anything else. I'll die. Nothing else, please.'

Pillai couldn't understand his language. He looked at the lawyer.

'Mister Pillai! Just play this one. If you won't, I . . . I'll die.'

'Pillai Sir, he's asking you to play *Santamu lekha* again.' The lawyer spoke quietly, not daring to disturb the silence.

'Again, *Santamu lekha*?'

'Yes, yes,' said Polska.

His head swayed with the music. The kirttanam came to an end.

'Don't stop,' Polska begged him.

'Don't stop, Pillai Sir. He's possessed. Go on playing.'

Again, that flooding sound.

Pillai played the kirttanam another five or six times. In the end, as if the sound became one with the silence, the music stopped.

Polska's head was still swaying. Like the resonance of a temple bell, his head, heart, and very self went on moving back and forth in the silence. Three minutes passed.

The lawyer let out a great sigh. Very hesitantly, he cleared his throat.

Polska turned towards him.

'Mister Aiyar, Mister Pillai. There's some kind of message in this. I hear a sort of wisdom, a message to me coming from some world. I am lost in that wisdom. I can't contain my excitement. It's truly a message, sent just for me. A message for the world. The message of your music.'

He was struggling to put his thought into words, smiling, innocent.

'Do you understand?' Polska asked.

'Yes, a little,' said the lawyer.

'I understand it well. No music in all the world has ever given me this message. I have received it with outstretched arms. No one, no art, no music has ever given me a message like the one I have just received. If you were to ask me to die now, I'm willing.'

'What is he saying?' asked Pillai.

The lawyer translated.

'Is he asking what I felt? Mister Aiyar, Mister Pillai! The whole world is littered with corpses. There's only noise, shouting, scuffling. A storm fells the trees. Waves rise up and engulf homes. Lightning strikes, and the trees on the road are scorched. Buildings collapse. Wherever you turn, a huge noise. In this battlefield, this tumult, I see only peace. Gradually, the noise abates; the roar of the deluge slowly fades away. A certain peace arises in my heart. The shouting, the clamour, the fighting can no longer touch me. I have risen above it all. To a great height, beyond the clouds, beyond the storm, where I don't hear even the slightest sound, where I have discovered peace, an undying peace. That is enough for me. Now I can welcome death. I am ready to dissolve into that peace.'

Polska spoke quietly. The lawyer translated again.

Pillai was astounded.

'Peace? That's what he felt?'

'Yes.'

'Really? Then isn't that what our Tyagaraja Svami has felt, the peace he sang about in this kirttanam with such yearning? Is that what this man, too, has realized?'

'That's what he says.'

'I didn't say a word. How did he find out?'

Pillai sat there, speechless.

'Mister Polska, this song also cries out for peace. But unlike the storm or the thunder that you spoke of, this song pleads for peace, for peace as the final goal.'

'Is that so?' Polska was entirely amazed.

'That's the message. Nadam, sound itself, speaks. It crosses all boundaries and delivers the message,' he said.

'Give me your hand. The hand that played the raga. Give me the fingers on which God dances. Let me have a whiff of God, let me kiss him.' Polska took Pillai's fingers and put them to his lips.

Pillai, too, received a message.

Note

1. That is, in the underlying acoustic intervals organized in a raga.

Alimony

The husband and wife were always quarrelling. Not a day passed without a fight. We were sorry that we took them as tenants. It's not even eight months since they came. So many quarrels! What is the grammar of fighting? It would be a fair fight if both parties beat up one another.

But these quarrels were not like that. He would beat her as if she were a donkey carrying a load of salt. She would put up with it as long as she could, and in the end, she would begin to howl. When a young woman starts to cry, you feel the pain; your stomach churns. You feel like getting up and cutting the guy to pieces. Can you call it a fight if you are moved to pity?

Just a year ago, this man had a forty-five-year-old wife. He used to live in another street. They say he beat her to death. It's just hearsay. Can one kill a wife by hitting her? People will blow things up. I couldn't believe it. But seeing what is happening now, I've started to believe it.

Two months after she died, he went to Kadalur and brought back an eighteen-year-old beauty. When he first came to our house, he had two young women with him. We thought they were his daughters. Later, we realized that one was a daughter and the other was his wife. I couldn't help feeling outraged. What a scoundrel.

The wife was tall, with a round face and a light complexion. I saw her braid—broad, thick, flowing down her back, as if her hair had been tamed like a snake. Not a wrinkle on her cheeks, her neck, her legs—she shone like a nugget of gold.

My wife said, 'Did you see? The Creator, God, clever as he is, must have made second wives particularly beautiful. I've seen so many like that. Second wives always look so charming. . . . You need to be lucky in everything.' She spoke with a mischievous smile. She wasn't referring to the girl's good luck but to mine. She herself is no great beauty and rather dark. From the day we got married, she's been feeling sorry for me.

'Such a girl—stuck with this old guy.'

Four months later, I asked that same question. I asked it when I saw her crying; she'd been beaten, her face was swollen, and her cheeks were bruised by the fingers that ground idli and dosai batter in that hotel.

The next day, my wife, Gauri, came back with the answer to my question. "'What can I do, Auntie? I lost my father. I lost my mother. My aunt twice removed brought me up. She was also alone. She was widowed when she was very young. She has children of her own. All the boys who came to see me asked for a huge dowry. Where could my aunt find that kind of money? I squeezed into this hole. It doesn't matter that he's old, but couldn't he keep me happy? I thought that most men would look after a second wife like the apple of their eye. It didn't work out like that for me." That's what she said.'

'Why does he keep on beating her?'

'For no reason. "If an old man has a very young wife, he gets suspicious. What else?" That's what she said in a nutshell.'

Four months later, the girl lost her patience. Whatever else was missing, at least she should have enough food. That was also absent. He never brought salt, tamarind, and rice on time. Half the time, there was no rice. Or else there was no chilly or tamarind. Every other day, she had only one meal. Who can survive on watered-down buttermilk and plain rice for three days, without any curry? He had his meals and coffee for free at the hotel where he worked, making idli and dosai batter. His daughter had married and gone away to her husband's home. And this crook was making a big deal out of feeding his wife, left at home.

The wife put up with it for a long time. In the end, she started talking back.

One day, it happened.

He came home from the hotel at 9:00 at night. He didn't see her. He went into the hall. She came in carrying a pot of water on her hip from the well.

'Where did you go?'

'Why? Can't you see I'm coming from the backyard? There was no water to scrub the utensils, so I went to fetch some.'

'It's only when I come home that this happens.'

'What happens?'

'We run out of water. You have a cough. You have to spit. You keep running to the backyard.'

'If they knew you were coming home, my cough, my spitting, would have controlled themselves. Even the water would have said to itself, "Let's wait an hour before I'm used up." Today, the water didn't know you were coming so soon.'

'What do you have there in the backyard?'

'There are four walls around the well. The landlord locks the back door at 6:00. What could be there?'

The girl was speaking loudly. In my mind I thought, 'Good for her.'

A few minutes later: sobs and groans. Then silence. It took me a long time to fall asleep.

The next evening, Gauri said to me, 'That girl doesn't step outside or even come to the door. She seems like a good girl. That monster beats her up all the time. How could one just take a girl and throw her into a pit? Even if her parents are dead, doesn't the aunt who brought her up have any sense?'

I said nothing.

'Today afternoon, she was lying down reading a book. Suddenly the old guy appeared. She quickly turned, as if she were coughing, and hid the book in the wooden trunk near her head so he wouldn't see it.'

'He started his interrogation: "What were you doing?" "Nothing," she said, "just lying down." "Nothing? Nothing? Really nothing? Really?" He pushed her into the corner against the wall. Then he grabbed her by the hair and pulled her to the trunk. "So what's this?" he said, pointing to the book. "You said weren't doing anything." Then he beat her to a pulp!'

'Was she reading some book she shouldn't be reading?'

'Just some book of stories. So what? Why should he stop her from reading?'

'He won't let her read?'

'Yes. In my grandmother's days, they used to say that if girls were taught to read, they'd write love letters to their lover boys. This old guy thinks just like that.'

'That's amazing. He won't let her read.'

'She was getting bored. She asked me if I could lend her a book. I gave her one. It's my fault.'

'Maybe she should have gone along with him. Did she have to pick up a book?'

'*Aiyayyo*. She said that from the moment of her wedding, she stopped reading. He strictly forbade her to read any book as soon as the wedding was over. So she resigned herself and never touched a book. Today she probably wanted to relax a bit by reading, so she asked me for a book, and I gave it to her. He never ever comes home in the afternoon, but today he suddenly appeared.

'Why did he come?'

'No special reason. Just to check on her. What she's doing, whom she's talking to. It was her bad luck that today, of all days, she happened to be reading. She's unlucky. Someone so beautiful—why does she have to be kicked around and beaten up?'

'Why don't you call her? I'd like to have a word with her.'

'She's not here. The wife of her husband's boss at the hotel came and took her to help make appalams. She hesitated, but in the end, she couldn't say no to her.'

'What if he comes to know of it?'

'I suppose he won't object. After all, she's his boss's wife.'

But the matter didn't end there. As soon as he came home at 9:00 that evening, he started a fight.

'Where did you go today?'

'Nowhere.'

'So you were here?'

'Why are you asking?'

'Your hands look as if they've made two or three hundred appalams.'

'Who told you? Yes, I did go to your boss's house. Did that crook with a monkey's face tell you? It must have been him. He had come to get the wheat flour. That monkey must have told you.'

'Why are you cursing him? He just told the truth.'

'Is he your CID spy?'

'Are you my boss's maid?'

'Does helping her make a few appalams make me his maid? What's all this talk? Don't we also need someone to help us?'

'But you said you didn't go anywhere.'

'Yes, I did. Had I known you had a CID agent in your service, I would have told the truth.'

'Why are you talking back?'

'It's you who are stirring me up, for nothing. What can I do if you pull the words from my mouth?'

As always, that mouth got slapped. Four or five times. Tears.

That's how that day ended.

The next day, she went to the boss's house and reported what the boy had said, and how she got beaten because of it. She added fuel to the fire. It seems that the boss grabbed that Hanuman and kicked him hard.

She came to my wife and said, 'It's a good thing that boy got a beating. Just imagine, he made a big deal out of my going to the boss's house. Maybe he'll wise up and stop telling tales.'

Four days later, Hanuman was passing by the house. Kalyani—that's the girl's name—called out to him and warned him to be careful. 'Stop tattling on others. I'll tear you to shreds.'

Hanuman evened the score. 'It's dangerous to listen to your old man. Why would I come anywhere near you?' He was grinning.

Later, the old man growled at her, 'So everyone says you're a good girl. You've earned a good name for yourself.' He wouldn't let go of that incident.

'Wait a minute. So I went to help her make appalams. That kid, the monkey, reported it to you. You made a big deal of it and beat me up. Is that fair? That's why I went and told the boss's wife. When I heard that the boss beat the kid, I felt good.'

'It looks like you're too big for me. Living with you is going to be a challenge.'

'Look who's talking.'

'Oh yeah?'

'You don't bring home even tamarind or chilli. Somehow, I get through my days and I'm at my wit's end. If you ate at home, you'd know how well your wife cooks, and you'd know all the problems of running the house. And you have the nerve to say that living with me is a challenge.'

'So you think living with me is the challenge?'

'Whatever.'

'So go away if you want to. I'll pay you alimony. Get out.'

'Alimony? What alimony can you give me? A little tamarind? You can't afford even a fistful of mustard seeds. Some alimony.'

I was shocked when I heard her address him so rudely. But I felt like applauding when I heard her mention the tamarind.

One day, a boy came and took Kalyani away to Kadalur. He said her aunt was ill. The boy was so out of breath, huffing and puffing about the aunt, that the old man couldn't say no.

One week passed. Then two, then four, then eight. Kalyani didn't come back.

After two and a half months, a letter arrived, addressed to my wife.

Madras

Respected Gauri Auntie, this is Kalyani writing. I hope you and Uncle are fine.

I'm now in Madras. My aunt is here with me. Auntie, what else could I have done? I know I'm pretty. Everyone says so. And I can sing well. I thought all this would be wasted. But I would have been content with some decent food and a few kind words. I realized that this would never happen. Some people here were recruiting actors for films. I was accepted. They have fixed my salary at 500 rupees a month. I'm thinking of sending him one hundred rupees each month to make up for his mistake in marrying me. When I think of him, I feel really bad for him. Sometimes I feel like running away from all this. But I've got into it. It's hard to get out. I have no wish to see him. That I'm able to pay him alimony doesn't seem right. But what should I do, Auntie? One mistake leads to many more. If my aunt had saved some money and married me to a young fellow . . . I don't know what to say.

I remember you often. Please come and stay with me when you and Uncle come to Madras. Please convey my regards to Uncle.

Yours,
Love,
Kalyani

My Good Father

Uma Shankari

I am the youngest child in my family. Two elder brothers came before me. I think my parents lavished care on me. Father also took me around, played with me, took joy in me. In Brahmin families, there were many dos and don'ts: 'Don't touch that,' 'Don't do that,' 'Don't stand there,' 'If you touch that, go wash your hands,' 'If you step on that, go wash your feet.' Whenever I questioned them, Father would take my side. He taught me how to look at the inner meaning, the essence, of all those rituals and customs. I also learned from him that we needn't proclaim our beliefs or non-beliefs, like a porcupine;

that the most important thing for people is to be modest and understated. He was not perfect. A short temper, various anxieties, desires, and weaknesses—he had them all. But all in all, understatement and a sense of calm and peace were his defining features, like oil floating on a pickle.

How did he come by understatement and inner peace? He had a natural flair for putting himself inside the mind of another person. That's how he was able to portray various characters as if they were alive and breathing. Moreover, it was as if a stream of questions was always flowing through his mind. Perhaps it breached old beliefs and brought new insights. It seemed to me that there was continuous questioning and making choices. Like in many of us.

He almost never helped any of us with our studies or asked about our marks. If someone asked him what grade I was in, he would ask me. Neither of my parents ever visited my school or my college. Whenever a cyclone hit Madras—and it happens every year—parents would rush to school to take their children home. My parents never came. I used to feel sorry for myself because of that. But when Father was posted to Delhi, I had to study

Shakespeare and Bernard Shaw in school; Father helped me with those texts. How did he know the meaning of so many English words? My own daughter used to ask me the same question. In hindsight, I think he did not believe in micro-management; I think he wanted us to be free to discover the world for ourselves. Freedom was very important to him.

Preparations for Deepavali in most houses began a month before the holiday. My girlfriends often got new silk skirts as gifts. Father would write four or five stories for the special Deepavali issues of the popular magazines, and with the little money he got for them, he would buy us clothes and crackers two days before the festival. There would be a cotton sari for Mother, khadi clothes for all of us, including the music teacher, the family doctor, and the maid. And no dearth of money for crackers, though I never saw him shooting one off!

Father used to sing a lot. He would hum for an hour or so while taking his oil bath. From childhood, he was formally trained in Carnatic vocal music under several gifted musicians. He had had special training in the compositions of Muttusvami Dikshitar. He was also fascinated and profoundly moved by the harmony of lyrics, feeling and sheer musicality in Tyagaraja's kirttanams. But he also loved Hindustani music and, in particular, the voice training that is

part of it. Occasionally, he would listen to Western classical music, too.

Music plays an important part in many of his stories. In an interview he gave, he mentioned his teachers with affection—particularly, Umayalpuram Swaminatha Iyer (USV) and Paththamadai Sundaramayyar (PS).

> USV was said to be in the musical lineage going back to Thagaraja. He used to take an hour to tune his *tambura.* He wanted 100% perfect tuning, without the slightest slippage. He saw life itself as music. He had a very acute ear. He used to ask us to pay attention to all kinds of sounds: a plate falling, noises from the kitchen, a cart rolling in the street. He used to ask us to see how close they came to the basic notes of the scale. This training awakened in me a new awareness of the subtle vibrations of sound, made me sensitive to the hum and buzz that is the universe itself (*nada pragnai*). PS, too, had great *nada pragnai* and treated me as a friend rather than a disciple. We should be grateful to God for being able to appreciate good music.

A sad incident took place when he was training under PS. PS used to come to our home twice a week or so to teach. Once, he didn't turn up for over a week, so Father decided to go to his house to check on him. While he was cycling to PS's house, he came across his teacher's dead body being taken for cremation. He was shocked. He learned that PS had been ill for a week and had suddenly died that morning. He scolded PS's son for not informing him, for he could have gotten him treated by a good doctor. Father came home in shock and slumped into a chair. I remember how he and my mother became sad and gloomy. Father said he would never sing again. And sure enough, he stopped practicing his singing with the tambura. But music did not abandon him. He couldn't help singing or humming casually. He sang when he was walking, bathing, and so on, and listened to music on the radio as well as attending concerts in Madras and in Delhi. In Madras, the radio was always on in the mornings. Always Carnatic music. Cinema songs blared only from neighbours' houses—from Radio Ceylon or Vividh Bharathi.

When he was a young adult, life offered him two paths: to become a writer or to be a musician. He chose the former. I think he was basically inward-looking and a little too shy to make a life as a performing artist, which also involved cultivating public relations, meeting patrons, and, in general, promoting oneself. I can imagine he didn't have the stomach for it. He used to say that music was meant to be experienced inwardly.

He put me in a music school when I was just five years old. I learned vocal music for over nine years,

but when we shifted to Delhi, I could not pursue it for logistical reasons; there were very few teachers, transportation was a huge problem, and so on. He wanted me to pursue my college studies in music, but I was thirsting to know about the world and took up sociology instead.

My mother was generous in her support to my father in his creative life and literary career. She read and appreciated his writings, welcomed and served the endless stream of relatives and friends cheerfully. One of his friends, M.V. Venkatram, paid a moving tribute to her hospitality when he stayed with us for an extended period. He was going through a particularly difficult time in his life.[1]

I can't say my parents' married life was one long, sweet love story. They had their quarrels. It had an effect on us children. But a week before Mother died, she and I had a long talk, late into the night. She said that Father had always valued her and treated her with great love and respect. I saw that she had forgiven him wholeheartedly. I was very moved.

For over fifteen years, Father worked for All India Radio Madras as a producer in the educational broadcast department. I think he loved that work. Every day he had to prepare an educational programme for middle-school children. Though the broadcast itself was only half-an-hour to an hour, he worked hard preparing it. It was his mission. Only rarely would he outsource it, and then only to some extraordinary persons. The broadcasts were meant to supplement the usual curriculum in many subjects; so he read widely, from science and nature to philosophy, literature, religion, and politics. I remember a play he wrote about Chanakya and another about Madame Curie. When I was in third grade, he was invited to my school as the chief guest on Independence Day. After he hoisted the flag, he made us sit around him. He did not give a speech; he told us a story—the story of Shibi Chakravarthy, a king who gave his flesh to a kite so that he could save a dove that had taken refuge with him. He deeply believed that education should not be a torture but a delight.

Once Father and I went to visit Vidya Shankar, the veena artist, at her home. She introduced us to an elderly aunt, who was blind. When Vidya said, 'Janakiraman has come,' the aunt got up from her chair. Father went to shake hands with her because she was blind. She hugged him and said, obviously elated: 'I have been hearing your voice for so many years!'

He spent another fifteen years, until 1982, in All India Radio in Delhi as the chief producer of educational broadcasts in the country. His last programme was on Bharatiyar and his quest for knowledge; he was planning another one on R.K. Narayan and Malgudi when he died, at sixty-one. He lived a life of intensity and passion, as if he had packed ninety years into sixty-one.

A few years ago, my daughter said to me, on some occasion: 'Mummy, there is a person whom you love deeply. You remember him eagerly. When you speak about him, your whole face lights up, and your voice chokes. You know who it is? Your father!'

Note

1. Ravi Subramanian in Kanali, 13 August 2020, http://kanali.in/anbi-narumanam/.

Glossary

agraharam: street or neighbourhood where Brahmins live
alapanam: elaboration of a raga
appalam: a dough of blackgram lentils flattened and sun-dried, dry-roasted in oven or fried in oil
Bhashanga raga: In the elaborate system of Carnatic music, there are parent ragas having all the seven notes; offspring ragas which may have all or some of the notes of the parent ragas; and Bhashanga ragas, which have one or more 'foreign' notes that don't figure in the parent raga
ceri: the street where Dalits live
CID: Central Intelligence Department
Gayatri mantra: a Vedic chant sung at noon and dusk in praise of Goddess Gayatri
Jadabharata: a sage famous for his innocence and his enduring silence

jangiri: a sweet named after the Mughal Emperor Jahangir

kalam: a measure used for paddy or rice

kirttanam/kirttanai: a devotional composition set in a particular raga and beat

kolam: a design drawn every morning with rice or white stone powder at the threshold of houses

kummatti: bitter apple

kumkum: vermilion powder worn by women on their forehead; widows are not allowed to wear it

kuzhambu: a soup of vegetables cooked in tamarind juice with other spices

nagaswaram: a pipe instrument, similar to the north Indian shehnai

nadam: pure sound

narmade, sindhu, kaveri sloka: a prayer to the seven sacred rivers of India, recited during bath

Pillaiyar: Ganesha, the god with an elephant's face, who removes obstacles

pitlai: sambar with ground coconut and jaggery

Rumani mango: a much-loved variety of mango with a smooth yellow skin

shruti: a drone of basic notes

sruti box: a small bellows-like instrument used to provide the drone notes

Svami/Sami: literally 'lord' but used to address a person of higher status

Takshaka: the king of the snakes in the Mahabharata epic

tali: sacred thread tied around the neck of the bride by the bridegroom

tambi: younger brother; also used to address anyone younger to oneself

tavil: a drum played as accompaniment to the nagaswaram

terukkuttu: traditional street play

Tevaram: poems to Lord Śiva that form the first seven volumes of the Tamil Śaiva canon; sung as part of the temple liturgy

tinnai: a raised platform on both sides of the entrance to a house used as a bench for sitting, lying down and other activities

vadai: a savoury doughnut made of black lentils, fried in oil

Vasuki: a great snake in mythology

veshti: a two-to-four-metre unstitched fabric wrapped and tied around men's lower body

Yama: the God of death

Copyright Credits

All stories included in this volume have been originally published in Tamil in the following publications.

'Temple Bell' ('*Kandaamani*'), in *Kalki*, 1966
'Alien Note' ('*Bhasanga ragam*'), in *Kalki*, 1966
'Offspring' ('*Santhanam*'), in *Kanaiyazhi*, 1968
'Debt Discharged' ('*Kadan theerndhadhu*'), in *Kalki*, 1950
'The Music Lesson' ('*Isaip payirchi*'), in *Ananda Vikatan*, 1967
'Payasam' ('*Payasam*'), in *Kanaiyazhi*, 1971
'Crown of Thorns' ('*Mulmudi*'), in *Ananda Vikatan*, 1958
'The Mendicant' ('*Paradesi vandhan*'), in *Amudhasurabhi*, before 1956
'Ecstasy' ('*Silirppu*'), in *Kalaimagal*, 1953
'Message' ('*Seythi*'), in *Sudesamitran*, 1955
'Alimony' ('*Jeevanamsam*'), in *Amudhasurabhi*, 1950